When Daniel James asks Jenni for permission to court her, she's not sure what God wants her to answer...

"Would you at least agree to continue seeing me while you make your decision?" Dan asked. "And, would you agree to set a time limit on this contemplation?"

Jenni sat back against the couch for a moment and considered Dan's requests. Surely there wasn't any harm in continuing to see him. She would have a chance to get to know him better that way. Maybe even lead him to a greater understanding of Christ. As for a time limit, that only seemed fair.

"I think I can agree to both of those requests," she finally answered. "I will give you a decision by the end of the summer. Is that acceptable?"

"The end of the summer?" he repeated.

"Yes. I'll have an answer for you no later than Labor Day. In the meantime, I would love to continue going out with you, as long as you continue to respect my beliefs."

Jenni felt proud of herself and grateful to God. She had managed to stand on her beliefs and it hadn't cost her Dan's friendship or his interest in pursuing his relationship with her.

"All right," Dan said after several minutes of contemplation. "But in the meantime, I'm going to do everything in my power to help you make up your mind." He grinned. "And I mean everything. I am growing rather fond of your company, Jenni Campbell. . . ."

TRACIE J. PETERSON is a popular **Heartsong Presents** author who often writes under the pen name of Janelle Jamison. She makes her home in Topeka, Kansas, with her family.

**Books by Tracie J. Peterson
under the pen name of Janelle Jamison**

HEARTSONG PRESENTS

If Given
a Choice

Tracie J. Peterson

Heartsong Presents

Dedicated to:
My sister, Karen.
Through thick and thin—sisters to the end.
I'm proud of you and I love you.

A note from the Author:
*I love to hear from my readers! You may correspond
with me by writing:*

**Tracie J. Peterson
Author Relations
P.O. Box 719
Uhrichsville, OH 44683**

ISBN 1-55748-589-5

IF GIVEN A CHOICE

PRINTED IN THE U.S.A.

one

"It's over, Jenni," Brian Givens said, getting to his feet.

For all her twenty-one years, Jennifer Campbell had never been more shocked. "What do you mean?" she asked, the pain reflected in her expression. "You're really going to call off our engagement?"

"I have to. I don't want to marry you anymore. I'm tired of competing with your God for attention."

"God? Is this about my faith again?" Jennifer raised a questioning eyebrow and pushed back her thick brown hair.

"You know it is. Your faith has always interfered with our relationship, right from the beginning. I want more Jenni, and you won't give me what I want." Brian's words were delivered without feeling or emotion. "I don't love you anymore, Jennifer."

Jenni felt as if she'd been kicked in the stomach. For over two years, she'd planned to marry the very dashing, very ambitious Brian Givens. She'd been the envy of all her friends, and even her family seemed to find Brian an acceptable candidate for son-in-law. The only questionable issue was Brian's lack of interest in God.

"You don't love me anymore? And just when did you stop? This minute, two days ago, last night?" Jennifer's voice nearly cracked. She couldn't help but think of the way Brian had held her the night before. He'd wanted her to come back to his apartment after their date. When Jennifer had refused, Brian had grown angry.

5

"You're just mad about last night," Jenni tried to persuade. "I thought you understood."

"It's not just last night," Brian retorted. "It's every night. It's everything! I can't further my career with a bunch of religious rhetoric—therefore, why bother? I've always taken care of number one, and I've never seen myself as a team player with God." His words shocked Jennifer as he continued to drive his point home. "You are such a naive prude, my dear Jen. A prudish, narrow-minded Christian. You know nothing of living, only of waiting."

"But, Brian, hasn't it been worth the wait?" Jennifer questioned, suddenly feeling uncomfortable with the turn the conversation had taken.

"You're the only one waiting around, Jennifer. I put aside such childish notions long ago. Too bad I had to satisfy my needs without you, but that was your choice."

Jennifer jerked her head up, and the flash of anger in her accusing eyes made Brian laugh.

"Surely you aren't naive enough to believe I've been faithfully waiting for marriage just to have sex?"

Jennifer grimaced. He made intimacy between two people sound cheap and insignificant. All at once, the revelation of Brian's true character came through the façade of what Jennifer had allowed herself to see for so many years.

"I don't even know you." The words escaped her lips. "But sadder than that," Jennifer said, staring blankly at Brian, "you don't even know yourself. You need God, Brian. Not as a team player, but as the Master of the game. You need salvation through Jesus Christ, or you won't even get to play the game!"

Brian ignored her statement with cool indifference. Instead, he brushed off his suit pants, re-adjusted his tie, and picked up his suit coat. "In two weeks we'll both be graduating. I'll take the bar in July, and then, well, who knows. It's an election year, and I have half a dozen people interested in bringing me on board."

"You'll be the successful lawyer and I'll be the up and coming young business woman. So why are you throwing away a perfectly good relationship—just because I'm a Christian and won't go to bed with you before we're married?" Jenni's voice was sarcastic.

"Sarcasm doesn't become you, Jen. Be a big girl about this. Go make your own way. You can have any kind of future you want. You can have it all!" Brian's brown eyes gleamed with greedy enthusiasm. Jenni began to wonder what she'd once found so attractive about those eyes. They suddenly seemed menacing.

"I can have it all—all but you," Jenni said sadly. She picked up her graduation cap and gown, and then she squared her shoulders. "Well, I guess the day wasn't a total loss," she said flippantly. "At least the Union got our caps and gowns."

"I'm sorry that you're so upset, but it's really for the best. I guess I'll see you around." Brian walked toward the Student Union.

Jenni gazed out across the university's campus and sighed. Everywhere around them were signs of the times: graduations, semester conclusions, and springtime love. Only the damp humidity of a Kansas day awaiting a seasonal storm made the world seem less than perfect. That and Brian's announcement.

Crossing the campus to the parking lot, Jenni felt hot, angry tears fall on her cheeks. Why was this happening? She'd always thought God had sent Brian her way. She'd even seen him as God's pet project for herself. Someone she could take to church and influence for God.

She unlocked the door of her car and got in. "Dear God, why is this happening to me? I love Brian so much, and now, now. . ." she sobbed. "Now there's nothing but the pain. I was so sure that Brian was the right one. How can I ever trust my feelings again?" She cried for a long time, but the question remained unanswered.

Jenni finally dried her eyes and headed for home. She pulled into the driveway at exactly five o'clock p.m., noticing the absence of her parents' car. Her father wouldn't be home for hours, and supper wouldn't be served until eight or nine that night, if at all. That's the way it went during an election year.

Jennifer was proud of her father. Keith Campbell was well known in the Kansas legislature as a real representative for the people. He was happy to try to live up to his reputation, and he did his level best to get out and meet as many people in the district as was humanly possible. "Unfortunately," Jenni sighned, "there's never enough of Keith Campbell to go around."

Jenni gazed up at the three-story house that her family had called home for nearly fifteen years. The houses on either side were stylish and affluent, but their home had its own Victorian charm.

She walked up the porch steps and paused, suddenly wondering what she should do next. Up until today, she'd planned to be Mrs. Brian Givens. Now she was just plain Jennifer Campbell. No purpose. No direction.

ॐ

Later that evening, Jennifer found a quiet moment to explain to her mother what had happened with Brian. Ann Campbell listened thoughtfully, throwing in an occasional question here or there. When Jenni felt that she'd said it all, she fell silent, waiting for her mother's response.

"I'm really sorry that you have to go through something like this, Jennifer," her mother said gently. "But I must say this, it's better for this to happen now, than after marrying the man."

"I know, it's just that it hurts so much," and with that Jennifer's resolve gave way to tears. Ann Campbell was holding her daughter, when her husband entered the room.

"What's wrong?" Keith Campbell immediately questioned, pulling up a chair beside his daughter and wife.

"It's Brian," Ann Campbell began. "It seems he doesn't want to share Jenni with God, and thus would rather not have her at all."

The angry look that crossed Keith Campbell's face was not seen by his daughter. His wife, however, knew that look only too well. Keith had never trusted Brian's motives where Jennifer was concerned.

Keith got up from the table and returned with a well-worn family Bible. Jenni expected to hear a verse about being unequally yoked with non-believers, or some other verse with the same theme. But instead, her father surprised her with another. "'If you are insulted because of the name of Christ, you are blessed, for the Spirit of glory and of God rests on you.'"

Keith Campbell read on and ended with a verse that comforted Jenni in a way she'd not thought possible. "'However, if you suffer as a Christian, do not be ashamed, but praise God that you bear that name.'"

"Praising isn't easy," Ann Campbell said as she pushed back a tear-dampened strand of her daughter's hair. "But our God inhabits praise. We must see His hand in this matter, and trust Him."

Jenni nodded, knowing her mother was right. "Thank you

for reading, Daddy. Thank you both. I knew it was right to talk things over with you."

"There's Somebody else you might want to talk things over with," Keith Campbell suggested with a glance heavenward.

"I know," Jenni replied with a deep breath. "I think I might owe Him an apology for doubting the wisdom of this decision."

Keith Campbell chuckled and lightly tousled his daughter's hair. "He doesn't always do things the way we think He ought to. That's for sure."

Jenni sat at her desk reviewing the verses her father had shared with her earlier. Reading further, she was encouraged to find yet another verse that seemed directed toward her situation. "So then," verse nineteen of I Peter 4, began, "those who suffer according to God's will should commit themselves to their faithful Creator and continue to do good."

Jenni thought on the words for several moments, before closing her Bible and going to bed. God's will had always been important to her, and now, when His will didn't happen to be *her* will, Jenni knew that this was the exact place faith must enter in.

She got into bed and breathed a prayer before closing her eyes. "Thank You, Father, for loving me, and for having an intricate plan for my life. Thank You for the blessing of good parents. Please watch over all of us, and help me to seek Your will as mine. Amen."

ᔥ

Two weeks later, Jennifer Campbell graduated magna cum laude, receiving her bachelor's degree in business. She stood laughing with her parents and sister, when Brian Givens and his parents passed by.

The atmosphere was strained, and Jennifer stubbornly

refused to meet Brian's eyes. Jenni thought she heard her parents breathe a sigh of relief when Brian and his parents moved on, but when she looked up to question them, they were all smiles.

"Come on," Keith Campbell said proudly. "I want to take this fine young graduate out to dinner."

"Can we go to. . ." Jennifer's thirteen-year-old sister Julie started to question and stopped at her father's raised hand.

"It's Jennifer's choice," he announced and Julie knew better than to suggest otherwise.

"All right," Jenni said as she consulted a mental list of restaurants. "How about the Dunraven Inn?" she questioned with a laugh.

"Not fair," Keith answered his daughter's suggestion. "It has to be in Topeka, not Estes Park, Colorado."

Jenni tried to pout, but couldn't keep a straight face. "Oh, all right, in that case let's go to Annie's."

"I like a girl who's light on my bank account. Annie's it is."

Jenni tried to enjoy dinner, but thoughts of Brian kept coming back to haunt her. She made jabbing stabs at her french fries, until her father placed his hand on hers.

"Jenni?"

"What? Oh, I'm sorry, Daddy," Jenni pushed her plate back with a sigh. Annie's had always served more food than she had appetite for.

"I wish I could make things better," her father said softly.

"It's okay, Daddy. Like you said, it'll take time."

"Yes, that's true. Time and space. It doesn't help to have to see Brian on occasion, and with the campaign year getting into full swing, Brian will no doubt be on the front burner."

"I know," Jenni sighed.

"Well, I'm glad you see it our way." Keith said, eyeing his wife with a grin.

Jenni hadn't missed the look that had passed between her parents. "What? Just what are you two up to?"

"Your mother and I thought maybe you should take a little time and get away." Jenni's father reached into his pocket and pulled out an envelope.

Handing it to Jenni, Keith Campbell enjoyed the look of surprise. "There's everything in this envelope to have yourself a nice three-week stay in Estes Park."

"Oh, Daddy, really?" Jenni fairly squealed with delight. "Honest and truly?" She reached into the envelope and pulled out reservations for her favorite resort, along with plenty of cash to enjoy herself during the stay. "This is just perfect," she said with tears in her eyes. "Thank you so much. You always know just what to do to make me feel better."

"I still don't like the idea of you driving across Kansas by yourself," Keith began.

"But, Daddy, I'm a grown. . ." Jenni interrupted but was cut short.

"I know, I know. Just hear me out. I have business in Denver on the third. I'll ride out with you as far as Denver. From there on, you'll be on your own. We'll arrange for your return trip when the time comes."

"Yeah." Julie chimed in with her thoughts on the matter. "You can fly me out and I'll ride back with Jenni." Everybody rolled their eyes at this, but Julie felt it was a perfectly legitimate offer. "Really, I could," she continued to insist.

"I said we'd cross that bridge later," Keith Campbell said firmly. "And if anyone flies out to ride back with Jenni, it will be another adult."

At this, Julie crossed her arms across her chest and heaved

a sigh. "I never get to do anything."

Jenni immediately felt sorry for her sister. "I promise," Jenni said, reaching over to pat Julie's arm, "I'll bring you back something real nice."

Julie continued to pout for a moment, but seeing her father's stern expression, she pulled her lower lip back in and straightened up in her chair. "Okay, Jen. But make it really, really nice."

"I will, Julie. I will."

two

Jenni followed the familiar scenic highway to Estes. The drive
up Elkhorn Avenue brought back pleasant memories of the
small romantic village. Here and there, Jenni saw her favorite shops and restaurants. The colorful congestion of people
told her that tourist season was in full swing.

Jenni drove through town and headed up higher into the
Rocky Mountains. Breathing deeply of the heavy pine scent,
Jenni felt as if she'd come home. How she loved this place
with its rocky grandeur and rippling river.

O'Reilly's hadn't changed a bit. It was still the same homey
looking resort that Jenni's parents had fallen in love with some
twenty years earlier. Jenni pulled up to the office cabin and
went in to register.

"Hello," she called out as she entered. She waited at the
entryway desk for the manager to appear.

"Hi," a young, red-headed woman greeted her. "I'm Amy
and I'm the manager here at O'Reilly's."

"Are you new?" Jenni asked curiously. "I don't really mean
to be nosy, but we were just here last winter."

"That's okay. I'm new all right. In fact I've only been here
for the last two months. I just barely got trained in time for
the busy season." The woman bustled around the office. Jenni
watched as she typed something into the computer. "Yep, here
you are. You have a reservation for cabin number eight. As
soon as this finishes printing out, I'll have you sign the receipt."

Jenni nodded and moved forward as the door opened

behind her.

"Jennifer Campbell!" a cheery voice called out, and Jenni looked up to see Pamela and David Walker, owners of O'Reilly's and friends of her parents.

"Aunt Pam, Uncle Dave," Jenni exclaimed as she was embraced by both. "How good to see you. I didn't know you'd be around."

"We came by to check on Amy, since this is her first season," Pamela Walker explained.

"Yes, she mentioned that. Will you be around long enough to catch up on all the news?" Jenni knew that her parents would want her to share all the latest information with their lifelong friends.

"You betcha," Dave answered with a bellow. He was a big man, standing nearly six foot-four, and he towered above all three women. "I want to know how your daddy's campaign is coming along. Is he facing any serious opposition this time?"

"Oh, you know Daddy. He considers every opposing candidate a serious threat," Jenni answered, the respect for her father's attitude ringing clear in her voice.

"And right he is to do so," Pamela joined in. "Now, Dave, let's let Jenni get settled in, and then we'll take her out to dinner. Dunraven okay, Jen?"

Jenni smiled and nodded. "You know it is, thanks. I can't think of anything I'd rather do."

Amy sat tapping a pen, waiting impatiently for Jenni to return her attention to registering. A look of dismay flickered across Pamela Walker's face.

"Amy, Miss Campbell is a guest of the resort. You should never rush a guest. We are here to serve, and that often takes more time than we'd like."

Jennifer whirled around, embarrassed by the fact that Pamela was rebuking her employee on her account. As she reached up to sign the receipt, Jenni dropped her oversized purse and out spilled most of the contents.

Pamela was reaching down to help Jennifer retrieve her things, when she spied a book among the mess. "Daniel James? I didn't know you read his work," Pamela said with interest as she picked up the book.

"I love his writing. His mysteries are always so intricate— I never figure them out before the end."

Pamela laughed and handed Jenni the book with the jacket picture facing up. "Not bad looking either," Pam added.

Jenni nodded in agreement, glancing down at the black and white photo of Daniel James. Jenni couldn't help but grin. "He's probably married with eight or nine children," she sighed.

Dave Walker let out a roar. "You're wrong, missy, wrong, wrong, wrong. Daniel James is as single as you are. And, he's coming up this way to rent number thirteen."

"Daniel James is coming to Estes Park? Here?" Jenni couldn't contain the excitement in her voice.

"Sure is, and I reckon you two ought to get introduced. Maybe he could autograph that book of his for you," Dave Walker answered affectionately. He'd always had a fondness in his heart for Jenni and her sister Julie.

After Pam enthusiastically agreed, Jenni allowed them to help her with her things and left them with a promise to meet them at the office by six o'clock.

ja

Later that night, Jenni sank down into the layers of blankets that dressed her bed. The veal parmigiana at Dunraven's had been delectable, and Jenni had enjoyed sharing Pamela and Dave's company. "Oh, Lord," she breathed a prayer. "Thank You for watching over me, and thank You for giving me understanding friends and family. Amen."

The following morning, a heavy mist draped the valley. Jenni was up before the sun, and finding it impossible to get back to sleep, she took a blanket and went out onto the balcony. Easing back into the wooden deck chair, Jennifer willed herself to forget about everything.

Jenni pulled the soft cotton comforter close, snuggling down to enjoy its warmth. Overhead, the twinkling of nighttime stars faded into a rich indigo blue sky, as the liquid gold of the sun peered over the snow-capped mountain range.

The rich green of forest pines were dotted here and there with Colorado blue spruce and quaking aspen. And as if the balance of blues and greens weren't enough, the mountainside was sprinkled with a riot of summer flowers. Blue columbine, white miniature daisies, wild primroses in shades of pink and lavender, all lent their beauty to the freshness of the new day.

As the sun broke over the mountaintop, Jenny basked in the warmth, feeling the damp cold of her body and soul give way to the sun's brilliance. For a moment, Jenni let her mind wander back home.

Her father would no doubt already be hard at work on his campaign. Jenni could envision him bent over a desk full of papers in the wood-paneled den that had become his home front campaign office.

Her mother would be in the kitchen making him breakfast and keeping a pot of coffee hot and ready for her husband's consumption. Jenni admired her mother for the devotion she showed her childhood sweetheart and husband. Jenni had hoped to show Brian just such devotion and care, but now that was a dream she must forget.

Thinking of her mother, Jenni remembered that Ann Campbell had always been there for her. There wasn't a time that Jenni hadn't felt important in her mother's life. God and family were the most important things in Ann Campbell's life, and Jenni had tried to pattern her actions after her mother's.

Sometimes she was more successful than others. Right now, Jenni fervently wished she could pray through her memories of Brian and the deep pain that filled her heart—and then have them disappear from her mind forever.

Jennifer was jerked back into reality by a noise on the ledge below her balcony. Looking over the edge, she glimpsed six deer as they walked across the resort grounds, hoping for breakfast hand-outs.

"Sorry, little friends," Jenni murmured as they caught her scent and headed toward the balcony. "I haven't got any food, and even if I did, the government says I shouldn't feed you." Realizing Jenni wasn't going to give them anything to eat, the deer moved on.

Soon the day was bursting into life around her, and Jenni decided to venture into town. She pulled on her faded blue jeans and tucked in a black t-shirt. Next she pulled on a warm, red plaid flannel shirt and hiking boot socks. Making her way to the mirror, she parted her hair and worked the brown mass into two thick braids. She pulled on her boots and grabbed her purse, and found herself feeling alive with energy. This was a good place to forget your problems.

She was just passing by the only telephone for resort guests, when she thought she'd better call home. The pay phone stood in a quaint, outdoor shelter with two stubby bench seats built into the enclosure. The structure had no door, but the short roof overhead was enough shelter from rain or snow.

"Jenni!" Before she could make her call, Pamela shouted to her from the office. Jenni gave a wave, and decided to put the phone call off for a few more minutes.

"I'm glad I caught up with you before you went to town."

Pamela came panting up the hill. "Amy quit on us and I was wondering if I could talk you into managing O'Reilly's." At the look of shock on Jenni's face, Pamela quickly added, "Just until we get another manager. The pay's not that great, but the benefits are. Room, board, Dave and I will see to the fridge being stocked, and there's the hot tub and free firewood. Need I say more?"

"Well, I wasn't really thinking of this as a working vacation," Jenni said thoughtfully. Seeing the worried look on her friend's face, she smiled. "I'd be happy to help out, Aunt Pam. Just tell me what to do."

"Oh, Jenni, you're an answer to prayer. An absolute answer to prayer!" Pamela pulled Jenni towards the office.

"Now, I don't care what you wear. I mean be clean, look well kept, but what you have on is fine. There are three cleaning girls that help out here. Kelly Johnson's been with us the longest, three years in fact. Then there's Gracey and Renea. They've both been with us through at least one season. They'll handle all the physical work, the cleaning, restocking of supplies, delivering firewood, and such." The older woman hurried around the office, trying to remember everything at once.

"Are you familiar with computers?" she questioned and then answered for Jenni before she could speak. "Of course you are, you're a college graduate. You'll probably find this a breeze."

Jenni smiled and tried to mentally reassure herself that Pamela was probably right. Fortunately for Pamela Walker, Jenni hid her feelings of apprehension well.

After Pamela showed Jenni the computer set up and how to access the software, Jenni soon felt competent enough to work with the system.

"I'm so grateful that you've agreed to help. I don't know how long it'll take to get another manager, but as picky as we

Walkers tend to be, it could be several weeks."

"That's okay, Aunt Pam. I don't have anything important to be back in Topeka for. Except," Jenni paused, "for the election. I really want to be back by then. I want to be there for my dad."

"Well, if I can't have a new manager for you by then, I'll take over the office myself. You just don't worry about a thing." Pamela gave Jenni's shoulders a squeeze. "I couldn't love you more if you were one of my own."

⁂

Five days later, Jenni waved goodbye to Pam and David. They had problems with another one of their many resorts, and Jenni was going to be on her own for a while. True to their word, they'd put in enough provisions to last Jenni the summer, and left two weeks advanced pay. Jenni had argued with them about the money, but Dave wouldn't hear of anyone working for him without getting paid for their efforts.

After taking care of two reservations, Jenni was happy to see Kelly Johnson coming down the path to the office. As Kelly drew closer however, Jenni noticed the frown on her face.

"What's the matter, Kelly?"

"You aren't going to believe what's happened," Kelly began as she pulled her shoulder-length blond hair into a ponytail. "Gracey and Renea quit. No notice, no nothing. They just quit."

Jenni's mouth dropped open in surprise. "Please tell me you're kidding."

"I wish I were. I have twenty cabins to clean." Kelly gave an exasperated sigh.

"What should we do?"

"Beats me, but we better do it quickly, whatever it is." Kelly headed for the back door. "I'm going to get the linens stocked up on the cart, and then I'm heading out."

"Why don't I help you? I'll take half," Jenni offered. "I'll put a notice on the door, and lock everything up. Then I can check back periodically and keep an eye out for new guests."

Kelly smiled. Jennifer sure was different from the redheaded Amy. Amy had never been willing to lift a finger to help the cleaning staff. "I'd love it! You can have cabins ten through twenty, they're the easiest. More modern conveniences and such."

"Sounds good to me. Just tell me what the procedure is," Jenni replied and locked the front door.

&

Finding herself smudged and sooty from cleaning fireplaces, Jenni began to question the wisdom of offering to help Kelly. The fireplace was the only truly dirty job, though. Given the class of clientele, most of the guests had cleaned up after themselves, and even the bathrooms were quick to mop and sanitize. The fireplaces, however, were entirely different.

Jenni was scooping the ashes into a metal bin, when a strand of brown hair pulled loose from her bandanna. Instead of pulling her hair into a ponytail as Kelly had, Jenni had tied on a scarf and left her hair to hang down in back. She was too late to correct the mistake at this point, and all Jenni could do was gingerly push the strand back in place.

Jenni continued with the ashes and was nearly done, when she heard someone come in behind her. Thinking it was Kelly, Jenni heaved a sigh. "I now have a greater respect for you," she began, when she was startled by the sound of a man's voice.

"I don't know what I've done to deserve such respect, but I do appreciate the thought."

Jenni whirled around on her heel, nearly dumping the bin of ashes. She lost her balance and plopped down hard on the floor. "Daniel James." She breathed the name with something close to reverence.

"I believe you have me at a disadvantage," the tall, blond-headed man said with a smile. "Here let me help you."

Jenni reached up her sooty glove, then quickly pulled her hand back. "No, I'll get you all dirty." She pushed the bin aside and quickly got to her feet. "I'm Jennifer Campbell, the temporary manager here at O'Reilly's."

Daniel James was immediately captivated with the smudged, delicate features of Jennifer's face. He studied her intently, as one might study a great painting, and after several moments of silence, he spoke again. "I'm very pleased to meet you, Miss Campbell."

"Please call me Jenni or Jennifer, but not Miss Campbell. It sounds too stuffy," Jenni laughed.

Daniel surprised Jenni by joining her in laughter. "I agree. I will call you Jenni, if you agree to call me Dan."

"I can't believe it." Jenni tried to take in every detail of the mystery writer. He was wearing black jeans with an emerald green, cable knit sweater. Beneath this was a cream colored button-down shirt, open at the collar. Jenni met his startling blue eyes and blushed, knowing only too well that he knew she had been sizing him up.

"You can't believe what?" he questioned with mock seriousness. Jenni could see a smile play at the corners of his lips. They were very nice lips, she noticed.

"I—ah," Jenni stammered for a moment, then regained a bit of composure. "I've read all your books. I love you—your work, I mean." Jenni felt the crimson return to her face. "It's awfully hot in here. I think maybe I've been working too hard."

Daniel laughed, a boisterous sound so loud that Jenni was reminded of Dave Walker. "You look as if you'd just finished cleaning all the fireplaces in the valley."

Jenni's hand went to her face; only then did she remember the sooty gloves. "Oh, no," she cried and went to the mirror to survey the damage. The image she saw made her feel like crying. Here she'd finally met someone she admired, and she was streaked and smeared from head to toe.

"Here, let me help," Dan said in a husky whisper. He had come to stand directly behind her, and when Jenni turned abruptly to face him, she nearly fell headlong against him. He reached out to steady her and smiled a knowing smile. If the smile hadn't been so intriguing and attractive, Jenni might have been offended at his seeming familiarity. Instead, she found his action stimulating. A shiver ran through her from head to toe, causing Dan's grin to broaden.

"First hot, then cold. Whatever direction will you run next?" he mocked lightly.

"The only safe direction," Jenni said with a smile, as she backed up toward the door. "Out of this cabin."

three

Daniel gave Jenni a few moments to compose herself before following her to the resort office.

"I'm sorry," he began, ash bucket in hand. "But you left this," he held out the bucket, "and I need to register for my cabin."

Jenni had already washed her face and brushed out her hair. With renewed courage, she took the bucket from Daniel's hands. "Sorry. I guess I'm just not used to meeting celebrities." She flashed a smile that warmed Dan's heart.

"All's forgiven, but on one condition," Dan stated with a grin. "You have to agree to have dinner with me tonight."

"Dinner?" Jenni was shocked.

"Yes, dinner," he confirmed.

Jennifer felt her heart skip a beat. "Well, I guess I could."

"Great!" Daniel's voice was enthusiastic. "I'll pick you up at seven."

Jennifer nodded and started to turn away, when she realized that Daniel was still waiting to register. "Let's see," she began, manipulating the computer. "You're in cabin number thirteen. We deliver fresh linens and firewood daily. Here are some maps and listings for local happenings—and last but not least, your key." Jenni handed Dan the cabin key; where her fingers touched his hand, she felt a spark of electricity go through her.

She tried to cover her reaction by quickly studying the balance of Daniel's bill. "You'll need to pay the remaining, ah, the remaining—balance," she stammered. "And sign the register."

Dan's eyes danced with amusement. He was finding this slim and pretty young woman to be most refreshing. She seemed so innocent and pure; rare qualities he had seldom encountered.

Finishing with the business details, Jennifer Campbell was almost relieved to watch Dan walk out the office door and up the hilly drive that rose behind the office. She caught herself watching him as he crossed the hill to his secluded cabin.

To her embarrassment, Dan stopped at the top of the drive and waved back down at her, catching her watching him. Jenni's face flushed a hot scarlet. "How humiliating," she thought, quickly averting her eyes.

Glancing at her watch, Jennifer was disappointed to see that the time was only one o'clock; she had six more hours to wait until dinner with Dan. She realized, however, that she had missed lunch. That at least explained the tremendous hunger she suddenly felt.

After a savory lunch of pasta and vegetables, Jenni returned to the business of managing the office. She was lost in computer records and guest receipts, when the first of the new guests began arriving.

Jenni was completely absorbed in caring for the guests, and when Kelly came in from her rounds, Jenni only had time to flash her a brief smile. Kelly, seeing that Jenni was buried in work, immediately went to the task of organizing the newcomers. She poured them complimentary coffee, then led them to the fireplace where they could sit and take off the evening chill.

The rush passed in a few hours, and after selling several additional bundles of firewood and handing out extra linens, Jenni and Kelly collapsed on the couch. "I never thought we'd get them all taken care of," Jenni said with a deep sigh.

Glancing at her watch, she was shocked to see that it said

ten minutes till seven. Dan would be coming to take her to dinner in less than ten minutes.

"Oh, no," she cried, jumping to her feet.

"What is it?" Kelly asked, leaning forward as though she expected to see something they had forgotten to do.

"Daniel James, the guest in number thirteen, asked me to dinner tonight."

"You certainly snagged him fast," Kelly exclaimed. She smiled. "I think I'm jealous."

"Don't be," Jenni moaned. "He's due here any time. Any chance you'd hang around and keep the office under control for me? I'll pay you overtime."

"Okay," Kelly said with a shrug. "I don't know why not. I haven't got a date with a gorgeous blond tonight."

"Thank you so much. I owe you one," Jenni said as she got up to leave.

"Just get me some cleaning staff," Kelly replied in exhaustion.

"That reminds me." Jenni stopped at the door to her bedroom. "Pamela Walker called, and she's sending us not two, but three girls to help clean."

"Well, that's an answer to prayer!"

"Do you mean that?" Jenni questioned. She realized that she knew very little about Kelly Johnson.

"I sure do. I turn everything over to God. I'd be lost without Him," Kelly admitted.

"I'm glad to hear it. I've missed fellowship with other Christians." Jenni braved the word "Christian," though she realized that Kelly could just as easily be involved in some other type of religion.

"Well, you're not alone anymore." Kelly smiled. "Now hurry up." She tapped her watch, reminding Jenni of the passing time.

Jenni flew around her room, throwing dirty clothes in one direction, pulling out clean ones from another. She realized she had no idea where Dan wanted to go to dinner, but that didn't deter her. Casual dress was pretty much welcome anywhere in Estes Park.

She surveyed her clothes and finally decided on a turquoise angora sweater and black slacks. She was just slipping on her black heels, when she heard Dan's voice in the living room.

Jenni searched the room for her purse, locating it at last just as Kelly knocked on the door.

"Mr. James has arrived," she called formally from the opposite side of the door. Jennifer thought she noted a bit of humor in Kelly's manner.

Jennifer opened the door and joined Kelly and Dan in the living room.

"Sorry, I hurried as fast as I could," she apologized to Dan, but he waved off her excuse.

"It's not a problem. Kelly was just telling me about your day."

He made an impressive sight, standing tall and lean in a black, western style shirt. The aqua trim at the pockets gave him a southwestern look. His long muscular legs were clad in the same black jeans that Jenni had seen earlier, and she was glad he wasn't a fussy dresser like Brian had been.

Brian! Funny, she hadn't thought about Brian Givens in days. Now, after all this time, when she did think about him, she was comparing him to Dan—and finding she already preferred what she knew of Dan James. *If only he were a Christian.*

"Did you hear what I said?" Dan's voice brought Jenni back to the present.

"I'm sorry. What did you say?" Jenni felt her cheeks flushing.

"I asked if Ed's Cantina was all right for dinner."

"Oh," Jenni barely murmured the word. "It's fine."

❧

Several hours later after a wonderful dinner, Jenni was sorry to see the evening come to an end.

"Dinner was great. Thanks for inviting me." Jenni had decided to keep the conversation light and impersonal, but Dan seemed intent on learning more about her.

"I'd like to get to know you better. Why don't we take a walk in the village?" He wasn't ready yet to lose her company for the evening, and he was searching for a way to prolong their date.

"I'd like that," Jenni said, realizing that she really would like to walk off the heavy feeling the huge Mexican dinner had left her.

Parking was always difficult this time of year in Estes Park, but soon Dan found a place and pulled in. He was out of his seat and helping Jenni down from the jeep before she could move.

"Allow me," he said with a grin. He gave her a slight bow from the waist.

"Thank you, kind sir," Jenni giggled. She was more comfortable with this light conversation. Tonight she had no desire to discuss the intimate details of her life.

Strolling down Elkhorn Avenue, Jenni pointed out some of her favorite places. "I love it here. See, down there is the Fudge Works—they have scrumptious candy. And over there is the Copper Penny—they have a lot of souvenirs and such, but I like the miniatures best," Jenni continued, her voice animated. "My favorite shop is the Cheshire Cat. I always stop there when we're in Estes."

"I know that shop," Dan offered. "I happen to love cats so I found the shop a long time ago."

"The woman that owns the shop is wonderful. She's very friendly and always has the most unusual gifts." Jenni added with a sigh, "I love Estes."

"Um, me too," Dan agreed. "That's why I'm moving here."

"Do you already have a house picked out?" Jenni questioned. Suddenly, she wanted to know everything about this man.

"Nope, that's why I'm at O'Reilly's. I'm going to start looking tomorrow. Maybe you'd like to help me."

"Me? Why me?" Jenni's voice betrayed her surprise.

"I don't know. You seem to have a real feel for the town, a love for the area. I thought maybe you could help me find something really special." Dan looked down at Jenni. He stopped momentarily to study her in the amber glow of the street lights.

Jenni grew uncomfortable under the close scrutiny. "Is something wrong?"

"Not at all. I guess it's just the writer in me. I find myself studying everything in detail," Dan offered.

Jenni tried to hide her disappointment. She'd hoped that he might say something special, something like he was attracted to her.

They proceeded down Elkhorn until Jenni remembered the attractive Fall River walkway. "Have you ever walked down by the river?" she questioned.

"No, I can't say as I have. But then, usually when I'm here, I spend a great deal of time in Rocky Mountain National Park, or climbing the mountains behind O'Reilly's," Dan informed her.

"Well, then, you're in for a treat," she said, and without thinking, she reached out her hand and pulled Dan along with her down Moraine Street.

Dan enjoyed the feeling of Jenni's fingers on his arm, and

when she dropped her hand, he linked his arm possessively through hers. "I kind of liked that," he said with a grin.

Jenni felt her heart beat faster and her breath catch in her throat. She said nothing, but catching sideways glimpses of Dan, she could see that he was smiling a self-contented smile.

Although other people were on the walkway, Jenni suddenly felt as if she and Dan were alone. Maybe the riverwalk hadn't been a good idea. She was, after all, still nursing her broken heart. One couldn't just throw away two years of marriage plans and dive into another relationship overnight. Or could one?

Dan seemed to sense her uneasiness. "Is something wrong?" he questioned, leaning down to whisper in her ear.

His warm breath against her neck made Jenni jump back. Seeing the startled look on Dan's face, Jenni turned away from him and faced the river. "I'm sorry," she apologized. "I guess I'm a little jumpy tonight."

Dan put his hands on Jenni's shoulders. She could feel the warmth of each finger as he gently massaged her tired muscles. "Too much fireplace cleaning," he said lightheartedly, and Jenni had to laugh.

Turning to face him, her laugh fell silent. They were standing only inches apart, and Jenni's feelings of apprehension quickly returned. What was it about this man that seemed to set her very soul on fire?

"Jenni, I—" Dan began, but Jennifer feared his words.

"We really ought to move on," she interrupted and began walking away.

Daniel stood fixed to the spot for a moment longer, a puzzled expression on his face. He ran a hand through his straight blond hair, then followed after Jenni. "Slow down. I want to enjoy this walk, not run a marathon," he said, coming alongside Jenni. He was careful not to touch her and left plenty of distance between them.

"I'm sorry," Jenni apologized and said nothing more.

Noticing her silence, Dan decided to move the conversation to a neutral subject. "So you like my work," he said casually and then felt like kicking himself. He hoped Jenni wouldn't think he was fishing for compliments.

"Oh, yes," Jenni said with renewed enthusiasm. She was relieved to find a subject they could discuss without stirring uncomfortable feelings inside her. "I really do. I've read every book that you've written."

"Well, not quite," Dan said with a mischievous grin. "I have a new one coming out this winter."

"Really? That's great! I'll look forward to reading it. What's it called?"

"Ah, well, it, ah. . .," his words faded into silence. "The title hasn't been decided," he finally announced. "Red tape and such, you know."

"Oh." Jenni shrugged her shoulders. "It's okay. I understand how red tape and bureaucracy works. My father is in the Kansas House of Representatives."

Dan perked up again. He was glad to have the conversation take yet another turn toward Jenni. "Tell me about him," he insisted.

"Well, he's really good at what he does. He listens to his constituents and cares about what they have to say. He's always getting blasted by the media for his moralistic stand, but it only seems to make him more appealing to the people. They trust him, and let me tell you, he worked very hard for that privilege," Jenni said with pride.

"I can well imagine. Public trust doesn't come easy these days," Dan replied with a hint of something underlying his tone.

"You sound as if you know all about it," Jenni said, hoping

that Dan would expand on his view of the matter.

"As a public figure, of sorts, I guess I do. People always expect certain things out of their heroes, if you can call both your father and me that. I just see what I do as a job. A job I love, true. But nonetheless, writing is simply the art and profession I've chosen to make a career out of," Dan answered thoughtfully. "Sometimes you don't measure up to what people think you ought to be. There are always those you disappoint, if for no other reason than the fact you're human."

"You sound a lot like my father," Jenni mused. "I think he'd like you."

Dan laughed at this but said nothing for a time. They strolled among the tourists and townspeople until the end of the riverwalk was in sight. "Should we cross over to the other side for the return trip?" Dan questioned.

"Why not?" Jenni said with a smile.

Dan could no longer stand the distance between them. When they got to the top of the bridge, he reached out and stopped Jenni. "Make a wish?" he asked offering her a dime.

Jenni laughed. "It's been a long time since I did that." She took the offered dime and thought for a moment. After closing her eyes, she hurled the dime into the rippling waters beneath them. For several minutes she continued to stand, watching the icy mountain river as it plunged over rocks and falls along it's way toward Lake Estes.

"What did you wish for?" Dan questioned.

She turned and looked at him thoughtfully for a moment, then grinned. "You know better than to ask."

Before either one realized what was happening, Dan stepped forward and took Jenni in his arms. As his lips lowered to hers, Jenni felt a strange surge of anxiety. *What if Daniel felt the same way about Christianity that Brian had?* Daniel had revealed very little about himself, and Jenni began to dread being alone with this handsome stranger. She couldn't let herself make the same mistake she had with Brian.

Jenni pushed away and turned to the bridge rail. "I'm sorry. I can't. Not yet."

Daniel's hands were on her shoulders, slowly turning her back around to face him. Jenni began to tremble and lowered her face.

"Jenni." Daniel whispered her name as he lifted her face to meet his gaze. "Who hurt you?"

Jenni sighed and relaxed a bit. "A boy back home. Actually a man, back home. A very cold-hearted man, who hates my religious views and prudish attitude." Jenni found herself spilling the entire story to Daniel.

"Sounds like the makings of a good novel," Dan said, trying to sound light-hearted.

"It wasn't the makings of anything good. That was the problem." Jennifer's voice cracked slightly, and she turned away from Dan once again. She could feel tears forming in her eyes, and she refused to let him see her cry.

"It'll be okay, Jennifer." Daniel spoke her name with such tenderness that she felt strengthened.

"I know," she agreed and turned to resume their walk. "If I couldn't count on that, I'd be hurting even more than I do."

As they walked back to the jeep, Jenni decided she had to face facts head on. "Dan," she began. "I have to ask you a question."

"Go on," he said, suddenly very serious. "What do you want to know?"

"After everything I've told you tonight, I mean my past relationship with Brian and such, I feel like I need to understand some things."

"I'm not sure what you're getting at," Daniel said uncomfortably.

"I'd like to know how you feel about God," Jenni stated bluntly.

"God? Is that what this is about?" Daniel tried to laugh, but his voice sounded stilted.

"Yes." Jenni paused beside Dan's red jeep. "I need to know."

"I see." Dan seemed to be considering the situation for a moment. He helped Jenni into the jeep and walked around to get behind the wheel. "I'm not sure I can answer that question. At least not the way you want me to."

"I just want the truth. Do you believe in God? Are you a Christian? Do you read the Bible and pray?" Jenni knew she was pushing too hard, but she couldn't seem to stop herself. After all, if he were a Christian, surely she would have been able to tell from the books he had written.

"Sure," he said at last. "I believe in God. I don't think you can come to a place like this and not believe in God." Dan started the engine and headed down the road.

Jenni kept waiting for him to say something else, and when he didn't, she felt compelled to press him for more. "That doesn't really answer my question," she said softly.

"No," Daniel said through clenched teeth. "I suppose it doesn't."

four

Dressing for bed, Jenni couldn't help but remember the cool dismissal she'd received from Dan when they'd returned to O'Reilly's. He'd been kind and polite, but nothing else. No tenderness, no request for another date, nothing. He'd not even brought up his request for her to help him house hunt.

"Lord," Jennifer found herself breathing a silent prayer. "Show me what to do. I just can't go through another tug-of-war relationship over my love of You. I guess I'd rather be alone."

Jenni thought about her words for a moment. Did she really mean that? Would she rather remain single than have to diminish or even end her relationship with God?

"Yes," she said aloud. "Yes, Lord, I do mean it." Somehow, just coming to that realization gave Jenni a great amount of peace.

❧

The next day dawned bright and clear, with Jenni's alarm clearly sounding at six a.m. The office would technically be closed until eight, but Jenni was quickly learning that she needed to be up and ready well before that time.

Kelly pulled into her parking place at exactly eight. Jenni had asked the petite blond to join her for breakfast. Jenni had something on her mind she wanted to discuss.

"Well, I'm here, but that's about all I can say," Kelly said as she joined Jenni at the small breakfast bar. "I'm so frustrated, I could scream."

"What's the matter, Kelly?" Jenni asked, holding up a pot

of coffee at the same time. "Want some?"

Kelly went to the cart that held styrofoam cups for the guests and brought one back to the table. "My roommate is moving back to her parents' house. Now I've got to find someone else to help share the rent. I absolutely hate looking for new roommates, especially in light of the fact I'm only going to be here another eight months."

"Another eight months?" Jenni questioned.

"Yeah," Kelly answered, deep in thought. "I'm transferring to another resort next year. It's a promotion."

"What will you be doing?" Jenni poured the coffee while she waited for Kelly's reply.

"I'm going to manage another resort owned by the Walkers. It's in Dillon which is a lot closer to my family. They live in Leadville."

"Well, that fits right in with my plans," Jenni announced, taking a seat opposite Kelly. "I think it might also resolve your roommate problem."

"What did you have in mind?" Kelly questioned.

"First let's pray, then we'll talk," Jenni answered. She offered a brief prayer of thanks before turning to Kelly. "I'd like you to move in here and help me manage the resort. I've already mentioned it to Aunt Pam and she thought it would be great. I explained to her that I needed a backup."

"So you could date the handsome Daniel James?"

Jenni frowned slightly at the memory of the previous night. "Well, at least so I can get away from time to time," she answered thoughtfully and continued explaining before Kelly could question her further. "This cabin has two bedrooms anyway and it would also be a security measure. Then of course there's the new cleaning staff. I'll need to have you in charge of them and it just seems smart to have the management located here, under one roof, so to speak."

Kelly wasn't listening to the explanation with any interest. Her eyes were scrutinizing the dark circles under Jenni's eyes. "So what happened between you and Dan?"

Jenni sat back in her chair with a sigh. "Is it that obvious?"

"Well," Kelly began, leaning forward on her elbows. "I fully expected to come in here this morning and find you all sunshine and smiles. Instead, you look like you haven't slept a wink and the tone of your voice makes it clear that something is bothering you."

"Oh," Jenni said blankly. "I wish I could understand it enough to explain it all to you. We really did have a nice time. In fact, I think Dan was very interested in seeing me again, but. . ."

"But what?" Kelly interjected.

"But, I started asking him how he felt about God and he didn't want to talk about it," Jenni answered.

"Boy, you just jump right in, don't you?" Kelly said with a laugh. "I don't think I would've had the nerve to start asking a man about his religion on the first date. You didn't by any chance discuss politics too?"

Jenni had to laugh then. "As a matter of fact—"

"Oh, brother," Kelly said and rolled her eyes. "You didn't!"

"It's not as bad as you think. My father is a Kansas legislator. We just talked about him."

"Whew, what a relief. So what happened next?" Kelly continued the interrogation.

"Nothing and that's the problem. He barely spoke two words after making it clear that he didn't want to discuss his view of God. I doubt he'll ever talk to me again, much less ask me out."

"Why not just accept his friendship and see where it leads. Dan James is going to be here for a while and you'll no doubt run into each other. Don't let yourself get so serious about the man; just be his friend."

"You know, you're right," Jenni said, and for the first time since she'd offended Dan, she felt the burden lifted from her shoulders. "I'm way too serious about this. It comes from spending too many years as a fiancée. I think I've forgotten how to just be friends."

The bells on the office door rang, indicating that someone was entering. Jenni gave Kelly's shoulder a squeeze as she headed to the office. "Thanks, you've helped me a lot." Jenni had nearly gotten to the office when she said over her shoulder, "Think about my offer, okay?"

"What's there to think about?" Kelly stated. "I'll take it."

Jenni nodded and turned to greet her first customer of the day.

The morning passed quickly but without any sign of Daniel, much to Jenni's disappointment. The new cleaning staff arrived, but since Kelly was still working to train them, Jenni offered to help with the cleaning one more time.

Kelly wrote down something on a piece of paper and handed it to Jenni. There were only two cabins that she wanted Jenni to clean, number twelve and number thirteen. Jenni looked hesitantly at the piece of paper; the number thirteen was staring her in the face. Kelly nodded and turned back to introduce the cleaning staff.

"Jenni Campbell, meet Karen Fletcher, JoAnn Madison, and Kim Jenson. They will be handling all the cabins after tomorrow. Karen will have numbers one through five. Those are the larger cabins. JoAnn will have six through thirteen, and Kim will have fourteen through twenty."

Jenni noted that Kelly fell naturally into the leadership role.

"It's nice to meet all of you. I want you to consider yourselves answerable to Kelly. If she needs anything else, she'll come to me. I'm looking forward to working with all of you."

Jenni smiled, picked up clean linens for her cabins, and headed off in the direction of cabin twelve.

Cabin twelve was relatively easy work. An elderly couple had rented it, and they were scheduled to stay for a week. They hadn't even used the fireplace yet, and that meant two bits of good news for Jenni. One, she wouldn't have to deliver a new bundle of firewood. And two, she wouldn't have to clean the fireplace. After seeing to everything else, Jenni reluctantly headed for cabin thirteen.

She was instantly aware that Dan was gone. His jeep wasn't parked in the designated place outside the cabin, and the drapes were still pulled. Jenni knocked anyway, but when no answer came, she unlocked the door and walked inside.

She immediately noticed things about the cabin that she hadn't before: the knotty pine paneling, the natural stone that had been used to make the fireplace, and the pine log table and chairs that sat in the dining room. Here and there, Jenni saw more personal items.

She couldn't do much in the way of cleaning, as Dan had left many of his personal items around the cabin, and Jenni didn't want to disturb them. She gathered all the trash and changed the towels in the bathroom and kitchen. Before leaving, she checked the fireplace where she'd first met Dan. He hadn't used it yet. That was good, as far as Jenni was concerned.

Jenni was nearly ready to leave when she remembered the small trash container in the bedroom. She went to check it and found a Bible on the nightstand beside the bed. Opening the cover, she found it inscribed, "To Daniel, From Grandma."

Jenni closed it quickly as if it had suddenly grown red hot. What did it mean? Did Daniel read his Bible? Was he a Christian after all? Or had Jenni's talk last night stirred uncomfortable feelings? Maybe Daniel was searching for the truth.

Jenni decided that if Daniel did speak to her again, she wouldn't bring up the subject of God nor would she mention finding his Bible.

༊ৰ

Coming through the back door to the office, Jenni was immediately overwhelmed with the scent of roses. Kelly stood at the office desk with a smile that filled her face.

Extending a florist's card toward Jenni, Kelly couldn't help but tease. "I'll bet I know who these are from."

Jenni was in a state of shock, and she stood for several moments without doing anything but staring open-mouthed at the huge bouquet of yellow roses and baby's breath.

"Well, are you going to look at the card?" Kelly questioned impatiently.

"I, ah. . ." Jenni stammered as she took the card. "I can't believe it. There must be two dozen roses in that vase."

"Three," Kelly replied. "I've already counted them— twice."

Jenni opened the card and read aloud. "Jenni, I'm sorry about last night. Could we try again tonight? Dan." Jenni replaced the card and looked at Kelly. "I think I'm in shock, Kelly. Can you believe this?"

"Sounds wonderful to me. I can't imagine anything more debonair than a man who apologizes when you've been the one to offend him. That's class."

"That's scary," Jenni replied to Kelly's words. "I know Brian would have never thought to do anything like this. I'm not sure how to react."

"How about just accepting his peace offering and agreeing to see him again? That is what you wanted, isn't it?" Kelly couldn't help but laugh as she added, "Besides, if you don't want them, I do."

Jenni stepped forward to take the roses from the office desk.

"Oh, no, you don't. Brian only sent me flowers twice in all five years that I knew him. These are coming with me," Jenni said possessively. "But, I'll keep them in the living room so we can both enjoy them."

Kelly followed Jenni into the living room, where Jenni placed the flowers on the coffee table. "What do you think? Do they look all right here?" Jenni questioned.

Kelly eyed them momentarily before replying, "I think they'd look good anywhere." And Jenni had to agree.

Later that day, Jenni was working at the computer when the bells on the front door sounded. Without looking up from her work, Jenni called out. "I'll be with you in just a minute."

"Take your time," said Daniel's voice.

Jenni quickly looked up to make certain that her ears hadn't betrayed her. "Dan," she breathed and after several moments, added, "It's good to see you."

"Is it? I was hoping that you'd forgive me for my behavior last night. Did you get the flowers?" Dan questioned warmly.

"Did I ever! What a surprise," Jenni said and motioned Dan to join her in the living room. "See, I've put them here where Kelly can enjoy them too."

"Kelly?"

"She's the co-manager now. She's going to help me manage the resort, so I can have some time off now and then," Jenni answered, straining to keep her voice even.

A smile played at the corner of his lips, and his eyes seemed to ask a knowing question before his mouth formed the words. "Time off to see me?"

Jenni blushed and tried to swallow her heart back down to its proper place. "I'd like that," she finally whispered.

"Good. I'd like that too. Do you have time to sit with me for a few minutes? We can discuss what you'd like to do tonight." Jenni nodded and took a seat on the couch.

"I am sorry about last night," Dan said, joining her. "I guess you just kind of took me off guard. I was thinking about everything you'd said about your previous relationship and I guess I just worried that I couldn't measure up. You know, give all the right answers and be the right person."

Dan studied her for a moment. Jenni had pulled her long brown hair back into a ponytail, and even without the benefit of makeup, her cheeks were rosy from the time she'd spent outdoors. He liked the simplicity of her beauty, so unlike the society women he'd found himself with back in the big city.

Jenni grew uncomfortable under Dan's gaze, but she was learning to deal with his detailed study of things. Finally, he spoke and Jenni began to relax a bit.

"I'm glad we can start over." Dan's words were barely whispers. "I really like you, Jennifer Campbell, and I'd like for us to be friends."

"I'd like that too," Jenni agreed.

five

Jennifer planned carefully for her date with Daniel. They were going to a dinner-theater at the Stanley Hotel, and while casual clothes were acceptable even there, Jenni and Daniel had agreed to dress up for the occasion.

As she surveyed the clothes in her closet, she made a mental note to either do some shopping in the near future or send home for more clothing. Having only planned for a three-week stay, Jenni had brought mostly casual clothes. She was silently assessing the situation, grateful that she'd thought to bring two nice dresses.

Finally deciding between the two dresses, Jenni placed her choice carefully across the end of the bed. It was a black silky print with sheer chiffon sleeves of the same color. The neck line dipped modestly in a rounded cut, with silver lace to offset its simplicity. The body of the gown was princess styled, and the flow of the mid-calf length dress would only serve to flatter Jennifer's already attractive figure.

After showering, Jenni rushed around to find all the right accessories. She would wear her all-purpose black heels, but tonight she'd don silky black stockings. Next, Jenni chose a necklace with an antique silver rose pendant to set off the touch of silver at her neckline. Securing the matching earrings to her ears, Jenni set herself to the task of styling her hair.

She had just finished stepping into the dress, when Kelly knocked at the door. "Are you decent?" Kelly questioned from the other side.

"Sure. Come on in," Jenni called over her shoulder. She was trying to figure out what she could take to ward off the chill of the evening air.

Kelly entered the room and gave a whistle. "You're a knock-out, Jennifer. Old Daniel won't be able to keep from answering your questions tonight. He'll be too enchanted to do anything but cooperate."

Jenni laughed. "I'm not too sure about that, but thanks for the compliment. Did you get all moved in?"

"I sure did. Thanks for the afternoon off. I brought everything I thought I'd need and the rest I'll finish packing and send to my parents. They'll store it for me until I get settled in Dillon," Kelly answered with much satisfaction. "I'm glad you came up with this idea."

"Me too," Jenni agreed. "Now if I could just find a wrap to go with this dress, I'd be ready."

"I've got a beautiful linen and lace shawl. Just so happens it's black. Would you like me to get it for you?" Kelly offered.

"That would be wonderful. Are you sure you don't mind my borrowing it?"

"What are roommates for?" Kelly laughed and went to retrieve the shawl from her room.

Jenni gasped when Kelly returned and spread the shawl across the end of Jenni's bed. "It's perfect, and so beautiful. Where in the world did you get it?"

"It was my great-grandmother's," Kelly answered proudly. "She brought it with her from Ireland when her family immigrated to the United States. She was a young woman of twenty, with a new husband, and a baby on the way. She'd been forced to leave all that she loved in Ireland, because her husband felt he could better their life in the U.S. This shawl and several trinkets from her mother's home were all she could manage to bring with her as reminders of her homeland."

"Oh, Kelly." Jenni's voice took on a worried tone. "Are you sure you want me to borrow this?" Jenni gingerly fingered the material. "It's so delicate."

"Of course I'm sure. It's only a piece of cloth. Sure it's valuable to me, but only because of my great-grandmother. I'm not attached to material things."

Kelly's words halted when Dan's voice boomed from the office. "Is anybody here?" he called.

Kelly giggled. "Do you want to make a grand entrance or shall I just make myself scarce?"

Jenni grabbed her purse and the shawl. "I don't need to make an entrance—and besides, I want to properly introduce you two," Jenni said as she pulled Kelly along.

Kelly nearly fell headlong into Jenni, when Jenni stopped abruptly at the sight of Dan. He was dressed in a black tuxedo, complete with black tie and cummerbund. Jenni found herself holding her breath as she drank in the sight.

"You look beautiful," he complimented.

The words made Jenni's heart pound faster, and in spite of herself, she blushed crimson, her cheeks fiery above the black dress. "You don't look so bad yourself," she teased, trying to alleviate her discomfort.

Kelly's cough, reminding them of her presence, dispelled the electricity between Jenni and Dan momentarily. Gratefully, Jenni pulled Kelly forward. "You two haven't had much of an introduction. Dan James, this is Kelly Johnson. She's now a co-manager, as well as cleaning staff supervisor."

Kelly laughed as she shook Dan's hand. "It all sounds very impressive, but it just means that I'm caught in the middle. If the cleaning staff doesn't clean I'll be the one to hear about it. If the paychecks aren't in I'll hear about that too. Either way, I'm in the middle."

Dan laughed at the animated blond. She was charming and very likeable. "I'm pleased to met you, Miss Johnson. We hardly had a chance to talk last night."

"Miss Johnson?" Kelly frowned. "Couldn't we be on a first name basis? I mean, I won't make you take me to dinner or anything." Dan's face creased with laughter at this, and Jenni couldn't help but join in.

"Kelly, I'm very pleased to be on a first name basis with you. Now, since Jenni tells me you'll be sharing this cabin with her, I'll have to get you to tell me all about her."

Kelly's eyes darted to Jenni, and with a mischievous grin, she said, "Now, that will cost you dinner."

At this they all laughed, and Jenni was grateful for Kelly's ability to break the tension.

Daniel reached forward and helped Jenni with the shawl. "If you're ready, I'll assist you with your wrap and escort you to the limousine," he said with feigned formality.

"Limousine!" Jenni gasped. "Surely you didn't—"

"Relax," Dan interrupted. "I just meant the jeep limo."

Relief washed over Jenni's face. "I'm glad," she replied as Dan lead her to the door.

"You two kids behave. Drive carefully, and don't give rides to strangers," Kelly called after them in a motherly fashion.

"She needs to get out more," Dan teased, and Jenni just laughed.

The drive to the Stanley wasn't far, but it was scenic, and Jenni enjoyed it immensely. As they drove east on the wooded stretch of highway, the Stanley Hotel's impressive structure came into view. Jenni had been there several times with her parents, but the massive white mansion hotel was always awe-inspiring.

In some ways, Jenni thought it looked out of place among the rustic, rugged mountains. But in other ways, she couldn't have imagined it anywhere else. From its arched windows, to its gabled peaks and flag-crowned tower, the Stanley Hotel had been built for the sheer elegance of pleasurable hospitality.

Jenni liked to imagine it brand new in the early 1900's. She could almost see the aristocratic lords and ladies, as they played croquet on the lawn or went for carriage rides on the grounds.

"You're awfully quiet tonight," Dan said bringing Jenni back to the reality of the moment.

"I'm sorry. I was just thinking about this hotel," Jenni said wistfully. "I think I would like to have lived in the days when it was new. I can only imagine the grandeur and splendor. If only these walls could talk."

"Now you're starting to sound like a writer," Dan laughed.

Once inside, Jenni and Dan were treated royally and quickly shown to their table in the MacGregor Room. Dan leaned across the table toward Jenni. "I can't help but compliment you again. You truly look stunning, Jennifer."

Dan's low whisper excited her, and Jenni found her voice shaky as she tried to reply her thanks. Dan James wasn't supposed to affect her this way, she chided herself. But she could not deny that he had a way with her that left her breathless.

"Are you all right?" Dan questioned.

Jenni offered a brief smile and tried to concentrate on small talk. "I'm just admiring the people and the atmosphere."

"There you go again. Studying the details is my job. Remember?" Dan teased. "Fact is, quite a few books have been written with this hotel as a setting. I don't think I'm inclined to join my work to the list, at least not yet."

"You never know, Dan," Jenni murmured thoughtfully. "You might create a best seller. Better not write it off—excuse the pun."

Dan's grin broadened. "There's something about you, Jenni," he said, pausing for a moment to contemplate his dinner partner. "I can't quite put my finger on it, but there's definitely something about you that I find intriguing."

Jenni hid a look of disappointment. Intriguing? He might have said that there was something he found likeable or delightful, even enjoyable—but intriguing? The word made Jenni feel like one of his mystery novels.

"I've been around a great many women," Dan continued. "It just sort of seems to come with the international author image." He laughed nervously. "Then of course, my mother has been after me to settle down, but that's not the point," he said with a certainty that left Jenni wondering exactly what the point was.

One of the attendants chose that moment to arrive. "Would you care for anything to drink?"

"Hot tea for me," Daniel replied. "What about you, Jenni?"

"Tea sounds wonderful," Jenni agreed.

After the attendant left, Jenni couldn't help but return the conversation to where Dan had left off. "What do you mean intriguing?" she questioned.

"Ah, I've piqued your curiosity, eh?" Dan kidded and reached across the table to give Jenni's hand a squeeze. The action startled Jenni and sent a flow of charges throughout her body. Why did he have to effect her this way?

Daniel's blue eyes narrowed slightly as if trying to assess the situation. Was it excitement or revulsion that caused Jenni to flinch whenever he touched her? Looking deep into her hazel-green eyes, Dan felt certain that distaste for his company was not what made her pull away.

"I find you intriguing," he continued as if nothing had happened, "because you are different from most women. You aren't wrapped up in your looks, though you certainly have reason to be proud of your appearance."

Jenni blushed uncomfortably again and looked down at her lap. Daniel ignored her embarrassment and continued, "I like the fact that you aren't painted and powdered to the point that I don't know where you begin and the cosmetics end. I find it absolutely enchanting that you can sit here in your evening finery, looking every bit the princess in contrast to your ash-smudged fireplace scene from yesterday. But perhaps most of all," he said with a gleam in his eye, "I enjoy the innocence. Innocence that is clearly not put on for the benefit of appeal, but just comes naturally out of who you are." Daniel fell silent.

Jenni had no idea what to say. "I suppose," she began slowly, taking time to consider every word, "that I've never before received such high praise. Thank you seems inadequate, but I do thank you. I appreciate the fact that you felt comfortable enough with me to be honest." Jenni hesitated, thinking to herself that what she'd just said sounded vain. "I don't mean that like it sounds. I just meant that your words didn't sound rehearsed or phoney. They sounded truthful, as though you were speaking from your heart. Not like you were trying to give me a line."

"Of course I spoke from my heart," Daniel said, suddenly quite serious. "I never compliment lightly and I never give such an in-depth perspective without a reason."

"Ah ha, the catch," Jenni said in mock surprise.

Daniel enjoyed the game. "I suppose you could say there's a catch. It's really quite simple, however. I would like—"

"Are you prepared to order dinner, sir?" the waiter interrupted.

Jenni dug her fingernails into her sweaty palms. What had Daniel been about to say and would he continue now that he'd been interrupted for the second time?

"Jenni, do you like smoked salmon?"

"Yes, as a matter of fact, I do," Jenni replied, straining to maintain control of her voice.

"Then may I order for both of us?" At Jenni's nod of approval, Daniel turned back to the waiter and said, "We'll have the smoked salmon."

Jenni couldn't concentrate on the rest of the exchange between Daniel and the waiter. She was thinking about the things Daniel had said to her. Why did they suddenly seem so important?

"You're frowning," Dan said, touching her hand again. This time Jenni didn't flinch but merely looked intently at the larger masculine hand that covered her own.

"I didn't mean to frown," she whispered. "I was just thinking, wondering really. . ." Jenni fell silent and dared a glance into Dan's eyes. They seemed to overpower her even from across the table. "I, ah. . ." she stammered to speak, but the words refused to come.

"You want to know what I was getting at earlier?" Dan questioned without a hint of teasing in his voice.

Jenni lowered her eyes for only a moment and then returned them to face Daniel's intense stare. "Yes," she whispered, and although the crowded dining room was alive with noise and activities, she felt suddenly as though the whole world had gone silent.

"I suppose you might call me a bit old-fashioned," Dan stated softly. "I have my own notions about how things ought to be and why. I don't dally with women and in that I mean that I don't lead them on in order to take what I want and be done with them. I despise the type of man that uses a woman's emotional affections—and physical ones as well—purely to advance his own goals and aspirations."

Jenni knew that Dan was speaking of the few things she'd

told him about Brian. She said nothing, however, far too interested in what Daniel had left to say to be distracted by the thought of Brian.

"I believe in the old-fashioned practice of courting. Does that surprise you?"

Jenni found herself shaking her head. It didn't surprise her, in fact Daniel's entire personality seemed so comfortably familiar, rather like sitting down with a well-worn, beloved book.

"A great many women are surprised by it," Daniel continued. "I've found that most women have given up on the idea of being treated with respect and gentleness. They find that with the attitude and actions of many of their gender, as well as the men they're acquainted with, this notion has simply passed on as a memory of more genteel times."

"I find it refreshing," Jenni said without thought.

"Somehow, I knew you would."

For a moment neither one said anything. Jenni felt certain where the conversation was leading, but in her mind she wasn't sure she was ready to hear it.

"Jenni, I don't want to play games with you. I don't want to waste precious time, but I also don't want to rush you. My fear is that one morning I'll wake up and you'll be gone without knowing how seriously I feel about you."

Jenni swallowed hard, but the lump that had formed in her throat refused to move. She could feel herself begin to tremble, and she knew that Daniel must feel it too.

"I want to court you, Jenni. I don't want to just take you out for a good time, although I certainly plan for us to have a great many good times. But I want to form a relationship with you that leads towards a more serious commitment." At the look on Jenni's pale face, Dan smiled. "I'm not proposing, I just want you to consider my feelings on the matter. If you are to continue seeing me, accepting my invitations and such, I want you to know what my intentions are. I'm past the age of playing games. I want to get down to the serious business of living, and I don't plan to do it alone."

six

Several weeks later, Jenni had still not given Dan an answer. She could hardly believe, though, in this day and age of people living together and flitting from one relationship to another, that this man would come and make a formal request to court her.

"I don't think I get it," Kelly said, washing the breakfast dishes one morning.

"What are you talking about?" Jenni questioned.

"This courting thing. I mean, I understand dating—isn't courting the same thing?" Kelly shut off the water and grabbed a towel to help Jenni dry the remaining dishes.

"No, not exactly. As I understand it or maybe I should say, as Dan explained it, dating is nothing more than a series of shared occasions, with no other purpose than to have a good time. Dating involves any number of other people, as well. But when you ask to court someone, you make a declaration of interest in marrying that person. It isn't a proposal, but it's a promise to see only that person and to work towards engagement and lifetime commitment."

"I don't see anything wrong with dating someone," Kelly offered. "I mean sometimes I think a person should take things less seriously and just have fun. You sure don't want to court every Tom, Dick, and Harry."

"Exactly Dan's point. He's twenty-eight, has his career established, and is ready to consider settling down. The problem is, I'm not sure I am." Jenni's voice held a hint of sadness.

"So what's the problem? You just tell him you can't consider courting, but you can consider dating," Kelly said simply.

"I don't think he's interested in dating. He's dated a lot and after knowing all these different types of women," Jenni sighed, "he wants to court me. I know I should be flattered, and I am, but I'm also confused."

"I think it's ridiculous to expect a woman that you've only known for a short while to consider anything so serious," Kelly said somberly.

Jenni stood thoughtfully staring out the window. A heavy sigh was her only reply. She knew Kelly was right, but on the other hand, Jenni found herself appreciating Dan's honesty and bold declaration. Jenni hadn't had that kind of respect from Brian.

"Well, don't let me tell you what to do," Kelly said, pulling on her shoes. "I think you should pray about it and wait for God's answer on the matter."

Jenni nodded. "You're right of course."

Knowing that Kelly was going to take over the office for the morning, Jenni decided to take a hike. "If you don't need me, I think I'll pack a lunch and go for a walk."

"That sounds like a good idea. Just you and God," Kelly smiled. "I'll make your lunch while you get dressed. What do you want?"

Jenni smiled. Kelly had fast become her best friend. "I don't care. Just give me plenty in case I get lost," Jenni joked.

Half an hour later, Jenni headed up the mountainside behind O'Reilly's. She'd decided to dress in khaki hiking shorts, black tank top, and long sleeved, blue cambric shirt. On her back, Jenni carried a pack with a pair of jeans, knowing that the air could turn cool quickly. The pack had several other things, as well as the lunch Kelly had packed.

Jenni rechecked the canteen on her belt, and after seeing that it was securely fastened, she began to hike in earnest. After living nearly two months in the mountains, she was well acclimated to the thinner air. Even so, the climb wasn't a simple task, and Jenni took her time. She also began an on-going conversation with God as she climbed.

"I thank You for this beauty and the freedom to climb and move about as I choose. I praise You, Father, for this time alone with You." Jenni panted as she reached the first plateau. She paused for a moment to look down on O'Reilly's, disappointed that she hadn't climbed very far at all.

Another hour found Jenni quite a bit further. Her legs ached from the workout, so she sat down to study the landscape around her. It was strewn with many rocks and boulders, yet the vegetation grew lush and green. Off in the distance, higher up the mountainside, Jenni's eye caught sight of movement. At first her gaze revealed nothing, and then slowly the shadows took shape and became big horn sheep.

"How glorious, God. How absolutely wonderful," Jenni whispered in sheer delight. Then suddenly she heard a rustling noise. The sound came from very near to where Jenni sat and startled her so that for several moments she did nothing. Unsure whether she should sit still or move about and make noise, Jenni breathed a prayer for guidance. She sat frozen, waiting, while the noise grew closer.

Dan stepped through the brush and smiled. "Am I intruding?" he questioned and then laughed. "Of course I'm intruding. I should ask, do you mind?"

Jenni breathed a sigh of relief. "You scared me. I wasn't sure but what you were some wild animal."

"Sometimes I am, but I'm well behaved," Dan teased. "I am sorry that I scared you though. May I join you?"

"Sure," Jenni replied. "Pull up a rock."

Dan crossed the distance between them and sat down beside Jenni. She grew momentarily uncomfortable at his closeness, but decided to say nothing.

"Seriously," Dan began. "I have something I wanted to talk to you about."

"I'm not sure I want to hear it considering the last time we talked seriously." Jenni tried to make light of Dan's dinner proclamation.

"Well, this is completely different, although I'd like to know your thoughts on that matter too," Dan answered, removing his backpack.

"That looks like a good idea," Jenni said, ignoring Dan's words. Dan reached up and helped her take off her own pack. He placed it beside his, and Jenni stretched her arms high into the air. "That's much better. I hadn't realized how sore I was getting."

"You shouldn't overdo it, you know. Is this the first time you've been hiking since you've been in Estes?" Dan questioned.

"Yes, and believe me, it's been a humbling experience," Jenni laughed.

"Well, you shouldn't have come this far the first time out. You should get used to climbing and using your muscles. You'll probably be pretty sore tomorrow," Dan chided.

"Live and learn, I guess," Jenni said nonchalantly. She was relieved that Dan had apparently forgotten whatever it was he wanted to discuss. Her relief was short-lived, however.

"Getting back to what I started to talk to you about," he began. He leaned back on his elbow and turned towards Jenni. "I've been asked to speak at a fiction writers' conference here in Estes Park."

Jenni let her breath out slowly, not realizing that she'd been holding it. "That's good, isn't it?" she asked innocently.

Having never been to a writers' conference, Jenni could only guess that being asked to speak at one was an honor.

"Yes and no," Dan sighed. "On one hand it's great to be recognized and thought an authority in your field. But on the other hand, it becomes a terrible infringement on your privacy."

"I see," Jenni said thoughtfully. "So you aren't sure you want to accept their offer, because you don't want to reveal the private life of Daniel James?"

Dan smiled and raised a questioning eyebrow. "Would you want to reveal so much of yourself?"

Jenni turned slightly to study Dan's face before asking yet another question. "What do you have to hide?"

Dan's face suddenly sobered. His eyes seemed to narrow slightly, and Jenni couldn't help but note a change in his attitude. "It has nothing to do with hiding anything. It has to do with sharing the intimate details of your life with total strangers."

To Jenni's own surprise she found herself bringing up Dan's courtship idea. "Yet you want to share the intimate details of your life with me—and I'm a total stranger, or very nearly."

"You're different," Daniel said plainly.

"Why?"

"I told you why, don't play games with me. Not with something as serious as this." Dan's voice was stern.

"I wasn't playing games, Dan." Jenni returned his firmness. "I know very little about you and yet you want me to consider letting you court me with the ultimate purpose of marriage in mind. Now I ask you, just who's playing games?"

"What do you mean?" Now his voice was cool.

Bracing herself, Jenni ventured on. "I'm talking about our first date, Dan. I shared a part of my past, a very painful part with you, and then I asked you some simple questions about

God and you refused to answer me. I think if you want me to seriously consider being courted by you, then you owe me some explanation as to why you reacted the way you did."

"I just wanted to have a nice talk with you about this writers' conference—not set up a battleground over religious issues," Dan said as he sat up. The tension in his voice was clear.

"See what I mean? You're avoiding my point."

"I'm not avoiding anything. I just wanted to discuss this conference. That's all," Dan said, his voice less strained. "Honestly, Jenni, the conference will be held at the end of October and I have to have an answer for these people by the end of the summer. I just thought maybe you could offer me some advice."

Jenni got off the rock and reached for her pack. "Advice on what, Dan? How to avoid the issues? How to run from questions?"

"Jenni, that's not fair. I don't want to argue with you." Dan came to stand beside her.

His blue eyes were captivating, and Jenni felt her fortitude dissolve. Warning bells went off in her head, and she hugged her backpack protectively to her chest.

"I don't want to argue with you either, Daniel. I just want you to answer my questions," Jenni whispered against the mountain breeze.

"I'm sorry," Dan said, pulling on his pack. "I can't, not yet." Without waiting for Jenni to say anything, Dan headed back in the direction from which he'd appeared. There was a sadness in the way he carried himself, and instead of feeling angry with him, Jenni felt concerned. What was it that made talking about God so difficult for him?

By noontime, Jenni returned to the office. She'd devoured the lunch Kelly had packed, and found that her water was nearly depleted from her canteen. She'd have to plan more carefully next time, especially if she intended to get further up into the mountains.

Kelly was busy with one of the cleaning girls, so Jenni went to the office and began to update the computer information. The rest of the day was quiet, and by the time Kelly left for her evening off, Jenni was growing bored. Most of the guests were regulars who'd been scheduled for stays of a week or more and required only a minimum amount of attention from their resort manager.

Jenni switched on the "No Vacancy" sign and locked the front door to the office. Without giving any real thought to what she was doing, Jenni locked the back door and headed up the hill to cabin number thirteen.

Somehow, Jenni knew that Daniel would be outside. He was sitting back in the shadows of the porch, watching as Jenni approached. Jenni knew he was there. She could just barely make out his form in the twilight.

"I don't have a white flag," she called out, approaching the porch. "But if I did, I'd be waving it now."

Daniel's chuckle let Jenni know she was welcome to join him. "So you surrender, is that it?"

Jenni climbed the steps to the porch deck and took a chair beside Daniel. "Surrender? I'm not sure that I would have used that exact word." Jenni thought to herself that surrender was the last thing she had in mind, but she bit back any further retort.

"And what word would you have used?"

Jenni smiled to herself, and thought for a moment before answering, "Perhaps truce."

"Truce?" Dan said, acting surprised. "Are we at war?"

"Of course not," Jenni mused. "But I felt that I owed it to you, to both of us, to explain myself."

"Go on," Dan encouraged softly.

"Well," Jenni began slowly. "I can't explain what's really going on in my head or my heart. I'm afraid the past is causing me to be rather harsh with you."

"I'm a good listener. Why not tell me about it," Dan sympathized, and Jenni found herself expanding on her break up with Brian.

"I really thought he loved me. I thought we both had the same goals and dreams," Jenni remembered painfully. Then pausing as if to consider whether or not to say more, she allowed herself a quick glance at Dan's face. The darkness obscured the details and left Jenni wondering if Dan could really understand what she was trying to say.

"Go on," Dan whispered in a low husky tone. He reached over and took hold of Jenni's hand.

Jenni enjoyed his touch and tried not to think of what it would be like to be in Dan's arms. "I figured that if I was a Christian and trusted God, then everything that came into my life was by His direction. I thought it would be mostly good things. You know, blessings and such," Jenni said, hoping Daniel would reveal his thoughts on the matter. When he said nothing, she continued, "I believed that God would protect me from problems like this. I saw God as this great big shield. I figured He'd keep me safe from everything bad."

"And now you don't believe that?" Dan questioned in a noncommittal voice.

"I don't know."

There, at last it was out. Jenni knew that she'd been struggling with something deeper than Brian's painful exit from her life and Dan's reluctance to answer her questions. Her faith had been truly shaken for the first time in her life.

"I guess what bothers me the most," Jenni began again, "is the uncertainty of why things like this have to happen and when they will strike again. On top of everything else, you appear and ask me to let you court me. Even more important, you want me to give serious thought to sharing my life with you." At this Dan squeezed her hand. Jenni got to her feet and moved to the porch rail.

"All of this seems so out of control. For two years I thought I knew what would happen next. I thought I knew how I'd spend the rest of my life and why. Now, nothing makes sense. I'd like more control in my life than that."

"Control isn't always what it's cracked up to be. Sometimes it's nice to let someone else steer the ship, so you can enjoy the scenery," Daniel reasoned from behind her. "If you're always strong, then nobody else has a chance to offer you support. You're always alone, almost like you have to do it by yourself or nobody else will. After so long a time of rejecting people's bolstering, they'll stop offering. Then you will be alone, Jenni."

Jenni took a deep breath. "You sound like you're speaking from experience."

"It just makes sense. Nothing all that mystical to it."

"What about spiritual?" Jenni dared the question. "How does God figure in?"

"Who knows?" Dan answered in a rather brusque fashion. "Who are we to question what God does or doesn't do?"

"Is that your way of saying, 'Who can know the mind of God?'—or are you just trying to steer around my question?"

Dan came to stand behind Jenni. When he turned her to face him, the moonlight shone just enough for Jenni to make out the strained look of turmoil in Dan's face.

"Trust me, Jenni," Dan whispered and Jenni felt dizzy. "Just trust me."

"How can I?" Jenni murmured. "I don't know you."

"I'd like for you to know me. I think I've already made that clear." With that Dan lowered his lips to Jenni's and kissed her gently.

Jenni felt her arms go around Daniel's neck, and without thinking about what she was doing, she returned his kiss. Daniel continued to kiss her until she thought she'd faint from lack of air. Lacking any interest in stopping Dan, however, Jenni only gave a half-hearted try at breaking the kiss.

She heard Dan's soft laugh as he lifted his lips and ran his hand through her hair. Jenni was afraid to open her eyes, and her heart was pounding so wildly that she was certain Dan could hear it.

As Dan stroked her hair, Jenni stood motionless. She was enjoying his touch, and when his fingers began to lightly stroke her cheek and neck, Jenni felt her knees grow weak.

"Stop, please stop," she barely breathed the words. "I don't want to feel like this."

"You don't mean that," Dan whispered against her ear.

"Yes, I do." Jenni tried to sound convincing, but she couldn't find the strength to break away from Daniel's embrace.

"No, you don't," Dan insisted.

"No—I don't," Jenni agreed.

seven

The emotion of the moment only seemed to grow. It was like a fire out of control, consuming everything in its wake. For a moment, Jenni tried to consider what she was doing, but she abandoned the effort; thinking rationally was clearly impossible.

As Dan pulled Jenni back into his arms, she enjoyed the warmth that his embrace gave her. She could not deny that he could arouse a response in her, one that Brian had never been able to stir. But just what exactly did that mean?

Dan's well-muscled arms held Jenni securely, and when Jenni dared to open her eyes and look into his, she could see the same longing that she felt, clearly reflected in the soft glow of the moonlight.

A sudden desperation began to surface in Jenni's mind, a feeling that left her little doubt that she would soon cross a point of no return. Dan showed no sign of releasing her, and Jenni knew that if she didn't break away from his embrace soon, she might give in to her emotions and loneliness. Uttering a silent prayer for strength, Jenni firmly pushed away from Dan.

"I shouldn't have come here," she said as she walked toward the stairs.

Daniel immediately closed the distance between them. Taking hold of her arm, he pleaded with her to stay. "Don't go, Jenni," his words were hoarse with passion, and Jenni immediately felt guilty for her part in what had happened.

"I have to," Jenni said, breaking free of his touch. "What I let happen here was wrong. I don't know how I feel about anything anymore, but I do know that. . ." Jenni's words trailed off. How could she tell him that years of resolve and obedience to God's Word had very nearly been destroyed just because of an emotional and physical high?

"You know what?" Dan questioned seriously.

Jenni paused for a moment longer on the steps and then, shaking her head, continued to walk away. "I'm sorry. I can't explain it to you."

"Can't or won't?" Daniel questioned, following Jenni down the stairs.

Jenni felt her determination dissolve. _Well, Lord,_ she thought to herself. _I might as well speak my mind and then maybe Daniel won't even be interested in me anymore._

The heavy scent of pine smoke filled the air. Jenni knew that most of the guests were enjoying a fire to ward off the evening chill. The coolness of the evening began to penetrate her jacket, making her wish she were once again in Dan's arms. She longed for the comfort and warmth of her own cabin as well. Dare she ask Daniel to come there in order to explain herself?

"You haven't answered me," Dan reminded. His presence was overpoweringly certain, as he continued to stand beside Jenni.

"Dan, I want to answer you, but not here. I need some privacy and I need more than a few minutes to explain. Why don't you come down to the office with me?"

"If it's privacy you want, why not stay here with me?"

"Because I don't trust. . ." her words halted abruptly.

Dan tensed beside her. "You don't trust me?"

Jenni thought his expression was almost pained. She reached out her hand, placing it lightly on his arm. "I don't trust myself," she answered plainly. Glancing up to see Dan's response,

Jenni felt herself flush at the grin on his face.

"I see." His tone was rather cocky, and Jenni began to wonder if she could level with Dan about her convictions.

"If you aren't going to take this seriously, then I'm not going to talk to you," she said defensively. She stood on the verge of explaining her philosophy of life, and meanwhile he was enjoying her discomfort.

Dan reached out and took hold of Jenni by both arms. "I've never taken anything so seriously in my life. I'll come with you if that's what you want, but I can also guarantee you that if you want to stay here, I'll remain a perfect gentleman."

"No. It's not that I don't believe you, but I do need to be available in case one of the guests needs something," Jenni replied. She pushed back her long brown hair with a smile, adding, "And I promise that I will be a perfect lady, so you will be quite safe." The teasing seemed to ease the tension for the moment.

"Very well, Miss Campbell. Lead on."

ая

Jenni allowed Dan to start a fire, while she warmed a pot of coffee on the stove. She took off her jacket and draped it across the back of a dining room chair. Daniel was already making himself comfortable on the couch in front of the fire, when Jenni returned with the coffee.

A strained silence seemed to hang over them and once again Jenni found herself wondering if she was doing the right thing. "Before I tell you what I have on my mind, I want you to understand one thing," she began.

"Go on," Dan said rather suspiciously.

"I don't want this conversation to turn into a religious argument." Jenni saw Dan grimace momentarily and quickly continued to explain herself. "I have to say that, because what I want to say in regard to myself and what happened back at your cabin involves my convictions, but I am not using that as a way to coerce you into making some spiritual declaration."

"I see."

"I hope so, because it's very important that you do. I am not trying to find some kind of leverage with you and I don't want to offend you by sharing my faith with you, but my faith is the center for all my decisions." Jenni took a sip of the steaming coffee and then placed the cup on a small side table.

"Well," Dan said softly with a genuineness that warmed Jenni's heart, "I promise not to be offended and I promise to listen with my heart, as well as my mind."

"Thank you," Jenni responded. "I couldn't expect any more than that." Kicking off her shoes, Jenni tucked her feet under her and settled in for however long this conversation would take.

"I feel rather embarrassed about what happened at your cabin. I should never have come up there tonight. I knew very well that my emotional state of mind would fight to control what I knew was spiritually true."

"And what is that truth?" Dan questioned.

Jenni laughed nervously. "I'm not sure it's that simple. I mean, I know what is spiritually true, but I'm not sure how to explain what I need to tell you."

"Just take your time, Jenni, and do it however you feel most comfortable. You won't offend me, remember? So just say what you have to say," Dan encouraged.

Jenni looked across the short space between them. She'd purposefully sat on the opposite end of the couch, in order to distance herself from Dan. But even from this distance Jenni couldn't help but notice every detail about him. He was the complete opposite of Brian and yet both of them had common ground as well. Both were charming and successful, both carried themselves with an assurance that was attractive. Did Dan also share Brian's disdain for Christianity? Unfortunately, Jenni knew far too little about Daniel James.

"Dan, the reason I grew uncomfortable back at your cabin is very simple," she finally said. She'd concluded in a brief inner battle that the direct approach was best. "I believe in purity of mind and body, as well as spirit. I've believed the words of the Bible since I was a little girl. I believe that there is more to Christianity than just saying you're a Christian. I believe that it is important to strive after the image of Christ in our lives. Does that make sense? Do you understand?"

"I think so, though I must admit you make it sound pretty complicated," Dan answered with a grin. "Why don't you just simply say what you're trying to get around?"

Jenni grew warm under his intense stare. The look in his eyes only made saying what she needed to say that much more difficult. She'd never been able to discuss certain subjects easily and this was definitely one of those subjects.

"Dan, I. . ." Jenni buried her face in her hands. "I feel so stupid. It's hard for me to say this and yet I don't know why. Maybe I'm afraid of how you'll react and maybe I'm afraid of myself, but the fact is this. I'm saving myself for marriage. The rest of the world may think me insane, but I intend to be a virgin on my wedding night." There, it was out, and Jenni heaved a sigh of relief and raised her face.

Dan studied her for a moment. She looked so small and vulnerable that for a moment he did not comprehend the meaning of her words; then their significance finally impacted him. He sensed her despair. "Come here," Dan motioned her with his index finger.

Jenni felt defenseless and silently prayed that Dan wouldn't take advantage of her weakness. When she hesitated, Dan motioned her again. "I won't hurt you, just come here."

Jenni slid across the couch and allowed Dan to pull her into his arms. She felt as though she belonged there.

"Jenni, you amaze me. I'm proud of you and yet astonished," Dan said gently.

"Proud? Astonished? What are you talking about?" Jenni questioned as she glanced into Dan's eyes.

"I'm proud of your convictions and yet astonished that you've managed to preserve your innocence, especially considering that you've been engaged these last two years."

"My principles destroyed my plans for marriage," Jenni reminded Dan.

"If the relationship was solidly built, it wouldn't have crumbled over the issue of sex. Your fiancé should've felt honored to have a woman with such beliefs. There are a great many people who probably regret giving in to sexual pressures before marriage. Relationships built on sex have nothing but feelings for foundations."

"Then you understand why I pulled away from you? It wasn't a lack of interest," Jenni said boldly. "It was a matter of right and wrong."

"I do understand, and it only makes me more certain," Dan replied in a way that made Jenni wonder at his meaning.

"Certain about what?"

"About courting you. About us." His words were so simple and straightforward.

Jenni said nothing for a moment, but she realized that the peace of mind that she'd attained from being honest with Dan allowed her to deal with the courting issue in a whole new light.

"Are you still interested, knowing that I won't sleep with you?" Jenni questioned, pulling away slightly in order to study his face.

"It's because you won't sleep with me that I've realized I

was right in asking to court you in the first place," Dan said confidently. "And, I think I deserve to have an answer."

"Yes, you do," Jenni agreed. "The problem is, I'm just not sure yet. If we court each other, it demands a commitment of sorts. I understand that it's not the same commitment as engagement, but I feel that a decision of this magnitude merits a great amount of consideration."

"I understand, but I have two requests that I wish you'd give me an answer on," Dan said seriously. "And, I'd like an answer tonight."

"And what are those two requests?" Jenni questioned curiously.

"Would you at least agree to continue seeing me while you make your decision?" Dan asked. "And, would you agree to set a time limit on this contemplation?"

Jenni sat back against the couch for a moment and considered Dan's requests. Surely there wasn't any harm in continuing to see him. She would have a chance to get to know him better that way. Maybe even lead him to a greater understanding of Christ. As for a time limit, that only seemed fair.

"I think I can agree to both of those requests," she finally answered. "I will give you a decision by the end of the summer. Is that acceptable?"

"The end of the summer?" he repeated.

"Yes. I'll have an answer for you no later than Labor Day. In the meantime, I would love to continue going out with you, as long as you continue to respect my beliefs."

Jenni felt proud of herself and grateful to God. She had managed to stand on her beliefs and it hadn't cost her Dan's friendship or his interest in pursuing his relationship with her.

"All right," Dan said after several minutes of contemplation. "But in the meantime, I'm going to do everything in my power to help you make up your mind." He grinned. "And I mean everything. I am growing rather fond of your company, Jenni Campbell. Furthermore, I believe with my intentions clearly stated, that I have a right to try and sway your opinion."

Jenni laughed out loud. "You amaze me, Dan. You truly amaze me."

"Oh, my sweet naive, Jenni," Dan said pulling her close. "You ain't seen nothing yet."

eight

The weeks that followed fairly flew by. Dan had kept his promise to do everything possible to persuade Jenni to allow him to court her. Everyday he tried something new and almost always he surprised her.

"Are you ready?" Dan asked one day, as he appeared at the office desk.

"Almost," Jenni replied. She had promised to go with Dan to look at several houses.

"The realtor guaranteed me that I would find something I liked among this group. Of course, he said that about the last group too." The frustration in Dan's voice was clear.

Jenni finished her work and set a stack of papers on one corner of the desk. "There," she said with a smile, "now I can leave with a clear conscience."

Dan looked her over with a grin. She wore a plaid pastel sundress with pale colors that echoed the misty hues of an impressionistic painting. The white eyelet lace that trimmed the bodice was the only adornment to challenge the simplicity.

Knowing that Dan would have the top down on the jeep, Jenni tied a white head scarf on, then grabbed her clutch purse. "Okay, Mr. James, I believe I'm ready to assist you in house hunting."

Fully anticipating Dan's gentlemanly gesture of opening the door, Jenni was surprised when he took her into his arms instead. "You look wonderful," he said with a satisfied grin.

71

Dan's lips pressed lightly to Jenni's, and she couldn't help but sigh. "I could learn to like this."

"Learn? I presumed you were already enjoying yourself," Dan chuckled.

"Perhaps," Jenni said with a grin to match Dan's, "you presume too much."

"Maybe." Dan paused as if considering the situation. "Perhaps that means I should redouble my efforts."

"Oh, no," Jenni said, pulling Daniel out the office door, "don't you dare."

Dan chuckled good naturedly as she pulled him along. "Lead me where you will, Miss Campbell. I promise to behave."

"That'll be the day," Jenni replied. Dan helped her into the jeep, then leaned down and gave her a quick kiss on the cheek. "See what I mean?" Jenni said in mock disgust. "I can't count on you to behave for even a minute." Dan just shrugged his shoulders and headed the jeep down the canyon road.

The first address they were given was located on the south side of Estes Park, near Allenspark. Dan had purposefully decided to start with the house farthest from the resort. That way they could spend the day working their way back.

Pulling up to the simple brown cottage, Jenni picked up the realtor notes and read, "Two bedrooms, fireplace, one bath, small kitchen. Sounds perfect for a bachelor."

"Then I don't want to see it," Dan frowned.

Jenni laughed and stepped out of the jeep as Dan reached to restart the engine. "Come on, you might like it here," she said with a smile. "It might also be very cozy for a couple. The ad says, 'Great starter home.'"

"Well, in that case I'll look at it," Dan said with a mischievous twinkle in his eyes. "You just never know when I might be a couple." Jenni rolled her eyes and followed Daniel into the house.

Five minutes later, they emerged. "I can't imagine trying to live in that place with a wife. You couldn't have two people in the kitchen at the same time."

"It did say, 'small kitchen,'" Jenni teased.

"Small isn't an adequate word to describe what we found in there. I've seen more space in closets."

After looking at two more houses, Dan suggested they stop for lunch. "Why don't we have a picnic in Rocky Mountain National Park?" he questioned.

"Sounds like fun," Jenni admitted.

Dan stopped by the grocery store and picked up enough food for an army before heading into the park.

Jenni leaned back and reveled in the scenery. The mountain peaks spread out before them, the moraines alive with vegetation and wildlife. Deer grazed in the open spans of meadow grass between the glacier-carved boulders.

"I could stay here forever," she murmured. The thick pine forest rose majestically on either side of the winding mountain road. Jenni could barely see past the thick undergrowth that carpeted the floor of the forest.

She wasn't aware that Dan was stealing glances at her from time to time. He enjoyed watching her. She was almost like a child, so captivated and amused by the intricate canvas that nature had placed before her. He would've enjoyed writing her as a character in one of his books. Perhaps he still would, but he hesitated to share his find with the rest of the world.

His thoughts were interrupted as they approached a crowded picnic area. He was lucky to find a narrow spot to park the jeep. "Come on," he said, grabbing the grocery sack.

"Here?" Jenni said in complete surprise. "You want to picnic in this crowd?"

"Why not?" Dan said with amusement in his voice. "I suppose you want me all to yourself. Is that it?"

Jenni blushed at his teasing. She hadn't thought of it in those exact terms, but it was the truth. She did want to be alone with Dan. Rather embarrassed, Jenni lowered her eyes to the ground for a moment.

Dan laughed, and after shifting the groceries to his left arm, he used his right one to pull Jenni close to him. "You will never cease to amaze me," he whispered against her ear.

Jenni buried her face in Dan's blue cambric shirt. She felt frustrated that Dan could read her so well.

"Look at me, Jenni," Dan commanded gently.

Jenni lifted her face and found a tender expression on Dan's features. "Don't ever be ashamed of your feelings, Jenni. I won't make fun of you. Just be honest with me."

Jenni nodded. Daniel James was certainly unlike anyone she'd ever known.

Dan led the way down a wooded path, leaving the regular picnic area. He stopped beside a small grassy patch. "I'm sorry I don't have a blanket."

"That's all right," Jenni said, taking a seat on the grass. "God's already provided one."

Dan joined her and placed the sack in front of them. "Here you go," he said, presenting her with a choice of sandwiches. "Turkey and Swiss, or roast beef on rye. What's your pleasure?"

"Umm, I'll take the turkey," Jenni answered, reaching for the sandwich. Dan pulled it back in a teasing manner.

"There is a price for this lunch," he said seriously.

"Oh?" Jenni replied with one eyebrow slightly raised. "And just what might the price be for turkey and Swiss?"

"For turkey and Swiss, you shall pay a kiss," Daniel rhymed.

Jenni laughed aloud. "I should've expected that from a writer. What would you have said if I'd chosen the beef?"

"Never mind, you picked the turkey and now you have to pay." He leaned forward to embrace Jenni. The brief kiss was tender, and Jenni couldn't help but think how much she would like to enjoy those kisses for the rest of her life.

They ate in silence, enjoying the melody of the forest around them. Somewhere nearby, water rippled in a stream, making a hypnotic, soothing sound.

With lunch finished, Jenni moved closer to Dan and felt his arms encompass her. She felt her pulse quicken when he turned her in order to kiss her.

She had planned on nothing more than an innocent kiss, but she found herself lengthening the embrace with her own passionate response. A part of her mind warned against allowing the encounter, and yet she chided herself for worrying. After all, Dan knew of her convictions and feelings. He wouldn't compromise that; she trusted him.

Feeling Dan's hands on her shoulders, Jenni trembled. She felt her breath catch in her throat. Pressing closer to him, she was suddenly rudely awakened when Dan pushed away from her and got to his feet.

"We'd better go," he said, his voice strained. He picked up the sack and headed back to the jeep. Jenni watched him for several minutes and then finally got to her feet. She couldn't help but wonder what she'd done to offend him. After all, he had instigated the kiss. Mentally, Jenni contemplated the situation and finally joined Dan at the jeep.

When Dan said nothing and made no recognition of her presence, Jenni felt a tightness in her throat. She feared she might start crying, and she turned to stare out her side of the jeep so that he wouldn't see her face. Under one of the pines,

Jenni noticed a young couple wrapped around each other in an embrace. Their position looked embarrassingly intimate, and Jenni quickly looked away. In doing so, she caught Dan's eyes.

The look on his face startled her. She was almost certain she saw pain in his eyes. Jenni refused to look away, although everything inside her felt the need to flee. Dan reached his hand up to touch Jenni's cheek.

"I'm sorry, I should have never let myself get so out of control," he whispered. "I promise you that I won't allow anything like that to happen again."

"But, Daniel," Jenni began, "nothing happened. At least nothing that I didn't allow."

Dan clenched his teeth and the tightening of his jaw made Jenni only too aware of his building frustration. "Nothing happened this time," he finally said. "But only because I stopped. If we'd stayed back there even one more minute, I can't promise you that I would have stopped." Dan was the one that looked away this time.

Jennifer said nothing as she contemplated his words. The world made it so easy to go against God's word. She realized that her trust in Dan's ability to control the situation had been unfair to him. She had selfishly enjoyed their embrace, taking advantage of his self-discipline, no matter what it might cost him.

Although they had other houses to view, Dan drove back to O'Reilly's. They hadn't spoken since the park, and when Dan offered Jenni his hand to assist her from the jeep, Jenni could tell that the action was strained.

Kelly was fixing lunch, when Jenni passed through the house, nearly running to reach the sanctuary of her room. As she fell across her bed, hot tears streaming down her face,

Jenni wasn't aware of Kelly's presence.

"Jenni," Kelly called softly, "are you okay?"

Jenni didn't answer, she couldn't. She sobbed into the folds of her comforter. Kelly put her hand on Jenni's shoulder, but said nothing.

Jenni cried for nearly twenty minutes. She remembered the pain of losing Brian, the confusion of what to do next, and how lost she'd felt until Daniel James had come into her life. Now, Jenni worried that she'd lost Dan for good. Why had she allowed herself to play around with his emotions like that? She made it clear that she wouldn't go to bed with him, but was she leading him on by allowing the intimacy that had taken place in the park?

When she finally felt she could speak, Kelly was there to listen.

"Oh, Kelly, I made an absolute fool of myself," Jenni said as she tried to control her voice.

"Do you want to tell me about it?"

Jenni nodded. "Let's go in the other room, though."

"All right," Kelly said as she got up to leave. "I'm making some lunch. Want some?"

"No, thank you," Jenni said shaking her head, "but I would like some coffee."

They moved to the couch where Kelly set a mug of coffee. "Now tell me what happened, Jenni."

"I acted very foolish," Jenni began, "and now I'm afraid I might have lost Dan for good."

"Would it matter?" Kelly prompted, forcing Jenni to face her feelings for Dan.

"Yes, Kelly, it would."

"Have you fallen in love with him, Jenni?"

Jenni's head snapped up to look straight into Kelly's

searching eyes. Jenni was reluctant to allow her mind and heart to answer Kelly's question, and for a moment Jenni refused to contemplate the answer.

Kelly sensed her friend's fears, and yet she felt Jenni must deal with the issue. "You may not answer me, but you're going to have to answer yourself. You can escape everyone else forever, but sooner or later, you'll have to face yourself."

Jenni buried her face in her hands. "Yes, I love him," she sobbed. She'd known it for some time and yet couldn't bring herself to say the words.

"Well," Kelly began, "it's clear that he's in love with you, so what's the problem?"

"I don't know how to say this other than to just say it. It's the physical attraction. I want this relationship and yet—" Jenni's words halted abruptly.

"And yet?" Kelly pushed Jenni to continue.

Jenni sat back, and drew a deep breath. "I let myself get caught up in the moment. Dan kissed me quite passionately and I don't think I would have stopped him from going further, if he hadn't stopped us both."

"And now you're afraid that he thinks less of you?" Kelly questioned. Jenni nodded. "I think you're wrong, Jenni," Kelly said simply.

"What do you mean?"

"Dan thinks a great deal of you, or he wouldn't have stopped. He loves you, Jenni. I'm more sure of that than anything, and I know that he's just waiting until he's sure of your feelings for him to say so."

"I don't know, Kelly. Maybe his feelings are just temporary. Maybe it's just a summer fling. I don't really know who Dan James is. He could be leading me on and I wouldn't know it."

"What do his actions say? What has he already told you? You have to trust something, someone. You've prayed about Dan haven't you?"

"You know I have, Kelly," Jenni replied.

"Then trust God, if not Dan James. God won't steer you wrong and He won't let you down. Trust Him, Jenni. God will show you soon enough if Dan's feelings are surface only."

nine

The next morning Jenni was working at the computer when a delivery man entered the office door.

"Morning, I'm looking for a Jennifer Campbell," the young man said.

"I'm Jennifer Campbell. How can I help you?" Jenni presumed that her parents were sending more of her clothing. She hoped it would be some of her winter things, as often the evenings were cold, and soon fall would come and then winter.

"I have a delivery for you. If you'll sign here I'll bring it in."

Jenni took the clipboard and signed by her name. She waited impatiently until the bells on the door sounded, and the man entered carrying a huge bouquet of apricot and ivory roses. They were arranged in a large princess basket of ivory wicker, and on either side of the handle were apricot-colored bows, trimmed with lace.

"Oh my," Jenni gasped. "How beautiful."

"This isn't all," the man said as he set the flowers on the counter. "I'll be right back."

The scent of the flowers filled the air and Jenni buried her face in the middle of their glory. She was just reaching for the card, when the delivery man came back with two large white boxes.

"Where do you want them?" he questioned.

"I guess in the living room," Jenni said in complete shock. "What in the world is inside them?"

"Don't know," the man answered. "I just get paid to deliver them."

"Well, at least let me get you something for your trouble," Jenni said as she went for her purse.

"That's not necessary," the man said, walking to the door. "I've already been well paid for this delivery."

Jenni was stunned. What in the world could have possessed Daniel to send her all of this? Remembering the card on the roses, Jenni walked back to the office. She took the card from the envelope and read: "Roses are ivory, apricot too, I've acted quite badly, but I love you."

"I love you!" Jenni said aloud. "Daniel loves me!"

The bottom of the florist's card instructed her to open the larger of the two boxes first. Jenni ripped through the slick white paper, and removed the lid. Disappointment flooded her, as the box revealed nothing inside but a piece of paper. Picking it up, Jenni read, "This box is like me without you—empty." Jenni was touched at the sentiment.

She opened the smaller box more carefully. She could tell by the sound that there was at least something other than paper inside. Removing the lid and tissue paper inside revealed two items. One, a fine piece of white linen stationery. It had been folded in thirds and sealed with red wax. The other item was packed in yet another box, and when Jenni finally removed the wrappings, she found an exquisite crystal vase.

Taking the stationery and vase, Jenni went to the couch. She carefully broke the wax seal, and opened it.

Dearest Jennifer,

Your purity is precious like this French crystal, so delicate and unblemished. I was wrong to treat you the way I did. Please forgive me, and come back. I love you.

Brian

"Brian!" Jenni gasped aloud. She had fully expected that all these things had come from Daniel. She sat back hard against the couch, completely dumbfounded. Why did Brian have to re-enter her life now?

Kelly entered the office and gave a loud whistle. "That Daniel is something else. You should have disagreements more often!" Kelly joined Jenni in the living room.

Spying the boxes, Kelly couldn't help but ask, "And what else did Mr. James send?"

"Not a thing," Jenni said blankly. "These things aren't from Daniel."

"Then who?" Kelly questioned as she sat down across from Jenni.

"Brian Givens!"

Kelly's mouth dropped open. "You mean the guy back in Topeka that you were engaged to?"

"The same one," Jenni answered. The shock was written clearly on her face.

"What does he want?" Kelly couldn't help but pry.

"He wants me," Jenni said in an exasperated tone, "and for what purpose, I don't know." She then proceeded to tell Kelly about the notes and what Brian had said.

"Oh, brother," Kelly said as she cast a questioning glance at Jenni. "You aren't happy about it, are you?"

"No, I'm not happy about it!" Jenni exclaimed a little louder than she'd intended. "I don't want them and I certainly don't want him!"

"Good for you!" Kelly whole-heartedly agreed with Jenni's decision.

"So what do I do?" Jenni asked her friend earnestly.

Kelly got up and paced back and forth as she considered Jenni's predicament. "He must want something from you. Yes, that's it, Jenni. He needs you for some reason. Why else would he be doing this now?"

"Indeed," Jenni wondered aloud. "I suppose you're right, but how do I discourage this? I mean, I don't want to talk to him and I certainly don't want to see him."

"Send it all back. Call the florist and UPS and send it back to the man!" Kelly exclaimed.

"Of course," Jenni smiled. "How very simple."

"If that doesn't make it clear to Mr. Givens, nothing will," Kelly added.

Within an hour the delivery man had returned for the items. He was puzzled, but nonetheless he accepted the generous gratuity and carried the things away.

Jenni felt as though a burden had been lifted from her shoulders, as the truck pulled out of the resort drive. But, even with the things removed from sight, Jenni couldn't help but remember Brian's words. They seemed genuine enough, and Jenni had to admit they'd touched her.

Not until nighttime did Jenni realize she'd not seen or heard from Daniel that day.

She was just stoking a fire when Kelly announced she was going to bed early. "You sure you don't want to share this fire with me?" Jenni offered.

"I'd better not. I have to get up early," Kelly replied. "I have the weekend off, remember?"

"That's right, you're going to see your folks. I'd nearly forgotten." Jenni pulled a book from the mantel and plopped down on the couch. "I probably won't see you in the morning, so have a good time and please be careful. I need you here."

"Don't worry, I've been driving this route forever. I'll be fine. Besides, I've got the best of Co-pilots," Kelly said over her shoulder.

Jenni nodded and tried to settle down to reading. She had been reading Dan's last book for several weeks now, and she was surprised at herself that she still hadn't found the time to finish it.

Her position grew uncomfortable for reading, so Jenni grabbed a couple of throw pillows and propped herself up. She stretched out in her gray, fleece sweat suit and started to read. Within moments, however, she was sound asleep.

When Jenni opened her eyes, she was instantly awake. Sitting across from her was Dan James. He had apparently been there for some time, watching her sleep. As her fear was replaced by recognition, he smiled.

"I didn't mean to scare you," he began. "I see you've been reading again." He motioned toward the book and Jenni nodded.

"The author's a genius. His intricate style and obvious talent blend together to make delightful reading," Jenni smiled. "I've been trying to finish it all summer."

"I can tell you how it ends," Dan offered.

Jenni stretched and forced herself to sit up. "I don't think so," she grinned. "You might leave something out."

Dan chuckled at this and then fell silent. "I suppose," he said after a moment, speaking with some reluctance, "that I've managed to put us in one of those compromising situations again." The fire glow illuminated his face with shadowy amber light.

"So why are you here?" Jenni questioned softly.

Dan watched her for a moment and offered her a sad smile. "I couldn't stay away. I knocked but when nobody answered, I tried the door. Since it was open, I thought I'd come in and wait for you. But, when I looked in here I found Sleeping Beauty. I didn't know what to do."

"You should have awakened me with a kiss. Haven't you ever read the story?" Jenni teased.

"I've read it all right, but after he kissed her, they lived happily ever after," Dan barely whispered.

"True," Jenni said, as if contemplating some great truth. "I think I'd like that. Happily ever after has a nice ring to it."

"Yeah," Dan agreed, but said nothing else.

Jenni hugged her knees to her chest. She suddenly felt bold and talkative. She motioned Dan to join her on the couch. "You seem so far away," she began. "I can't take care of the mental distance, but the physical distance is easy to handle."

Dan stood up and paused beside the couch as if considering the situation. Jenni appraised his frame appreciatively. He was a handsome man, she could not deny that, but what attracted her even more than his looks was his tender and loving manner. *Almost spiritual,* Jenni thought to herself.

"Please sit with me, Dan. I want to talk to you."

He looked deep into her eyes momentarily, and then as if what he saw reflected there caused him pain, he looked quickly away. "I don't know if this is a good idea," he argued.

Jenni noted his inner battle, and yet she felt confident about what she needed to say. "I promise to behave," she said lightly.

Dan took a place at the end of the couch. "In that case, I'm at your disposal."

A log on the hearth suddenly crackled and sparked. When it fell against the other pieces of wood, the flame ignited in a bright blaze.

"Dan," Jenni began, "are you angry at me?"

Dan looked shocked. "Angry? Are you kidding? I'm feeling many things right now, but anger has never figured into it."

"Good, I'm glad," Jenni said, her relief clearly sounding in her voice.

"How could you believe I was angry at you?" Dan questioned.

"I didn't know what to think, Dan. I thought perhaps you felt angry with me for what I did at the park."

"That wasn't your fault," Dan remarked.

"Well, whoever's fault it was, I didn't stop it. . .," her words slipped into a whisper, ". . .and so you had to. I thought maybe you thought less of me, maybe even despised me," Jenni said honestly. She had no idea where she was finding the courage to say what she'd been thinking all day.

"Jennifer, I could never despise you," Dan whispered. The sound of his voice made Jenni feel warm and cared for.

"Then you haven't changed your mind about wanting to court?"

"No, of course not," Dan said, suddenly snapping to attention. "If I gave you that impression—"

"No, Daniel," Jenni interrupted, "you didn't. I just needed to know for sure, before I continued."

"That sounds promising. Please do continue," Dan requested.

"I've come to a decision," Jenni said as she rested her chin on her knees. Her hazel eyes glowed warmly.

Daniel thought she'd never looked more beautiful. He longed to tell her so, but he was afraid he might break the magic of the moment. Instead, he waited for her to continue.

"I would like very much to commit myself to a relationship with you. I've given this a lot of thought, as you well know," Jenni said softly. "It hasn't been easy, because I had to sort through my emotions. I didn't want to decide to court you because I was lonely. I also didn't want to court you without knowing more about you, but maybe that's what's best about courting. You get to know each other in a more dedicated way than when you're simply dating for fun. And, Daniel, I want to know everything about you."

Relief flooded Dan's face, and he sighed aloud as he fell back against the back of the couch. "I was afraid you'd never want to see me again."

"No chance of that," Jenni said saucily. "I like what I see too much."

Dan grinned broadly. Jenni continued to intrigue him. She was soft and innocent one minute and a wild fire consuming him the next.

"So where do we go from here?" Dan questioned.

"I was hoping you'd tell me," Jenni said with a grin. She moved toward him; although he knew she did not know how she affected him, Dan was visibly shaken as he watched her.

"Jenni, I. . ." he struggled to remember what he wanted to say.

Jenni leaned back on her knees, still not touching him. She was within inches of him, though, as she waited silently for him to collect his thoughts.

Dan sat up and put Jenni at arm's length. "Honey, you ignite a fire in me without even realizing it. You have no idea how sensuous you are."

"I'm not trying to be." Jenni fell silent as Dan placed his finger against her lips.

"Just listen. It's important to me that you remain chaste. It's also important to me that we see each other often and exclusively. I think the best thing we can do is be very selective in regards to our physical contact." Dan paused for a moment to take account of Jenni's expression. She said nothing, but the question in her eyes was clear.

"If this is going to work, I suggest we only kiss occasionally. I further suggest that we avoid situations like this. I want to treat you with the utmost respect and I know I'll have a better chance of that if I don't allow certain kinds of situations to develop. Do you understand?"

Jenni nodded, and smiled. "I think you're wonderful, Dan James."

Dan laughed. "And just why is that?"

"Because you care so much," Jenni answered softly. "You care about all the right things, for all the right reasons." But even as Jenni said the words a question nagged at the back of her mind. Did Dan love God?

"Well, I think enough said for tonight," Dan said uncomfortably. He wasn't used to intimate praise.

"I have one more thing to say," Jenni decided. She knew that this wouldn't wait. "Will you promise me something?"

Daniel eyed her suspiciously. He had a feeling that he knew what she was about to request. "I'll consider it."

Jenni swallowed and took a deep breath. "When you feel you can trust me, would you please share with me your feelings about God?"

Dan grimaced only for a moment, but his uneasiness was clear. He reached up and traced the outline of Jenni's cheek, then allowed his hand to fall to her shoulder. He looked deeply into Jenni's eyes and for a moment lost himself.

"Well?" Jenni pushed for a response.

Dan dropped his hand. "I promise, Jenni."

With that he walked out of the cabin, leaving Jenni to contemplate the situation.

ten

True to his word, Jenni noticed that Dan held a more guarded attitude when he was with her. He was pleasant enough company and always found ways to astonish Jenni with little meaningful surprises, but he was also making certain he held his distance.

With Labor Day a month behind her, Jenni kept waiting for the tourists to slow their steady stream into O'Reilly's, but such was not the case. She tried to alternate time between the resort and Dan, but the feelings that she'd come to terms with left her little interest in the resort. More often than not, Jenni found herself just going through the motions of her daily tasks.

Kelly had noticed Jenni's preoccupation and tried on several occasions to draw her out, but Jenni wasn't ready to discuss matters with Kelly. The nagging doubt in the back of Jenni's mind continued to resurface until it consumed most of her waking—and often her sleeping—hours. How could she continue to become more and more serious about Dan, when she had no idea where he stood with God?

Loading her backpack with food and drink, Jenni decided to spend the day in Rocky Mountain National Park. There were plenty of secluded hiking trails, and Jenni intended to see and speak to no one but God.

She slid in behind the wheel of the car and was startled to find yet another one of Dan's surprises—a note was taped to the steering wheel, with candy kisses lined up across the dashboard. Jenni removed the note and read:

Jenni—These kisses should be safe—Dan

Jenni would have laughed out loud if her heart hadn't been so heavy. Tenderly, she scooped the kisses up with her gloved hands, placed them in her backpack, and made her way to the park.

Rocky Mountain National Park never lacked life. Even though heavy snowfall had already closed Trail Ridge Road, many of the lower elevation valleys were snow-free. Snow in the higher reaches, however, had caused wildlife to edge its way lower into the valleys below.

After driving around the park, Jenni decided to follow one of the popular hiking trails back into the seclusion of the park. She followed the winding park roads to the nearest ranger station and told the ranger of her plans.

After receiving the older man's praise for the prudence she'd shown by communicating her plans to him, Jenni turned the car back around and found her way to her planned destination. She parked in the designated area, donned her backpack, and followed the well-marked trail across the valley.

Jenni knew this to be one of the easier trails, and she found she could maintain a steady stride with little effort. She paced her steps against the slightly increased incline.

The morning sun had warmed the air, and Jenni soon found her scarf and gloves too warm. She slipped these into her sweater pockets and reveled in the sun's warmth against her face. Everything around her took on a brilliance that was never noticeable from the car. A person truly needed to walk these pathways to appreciate the grandeur God had placed here.

The altitude began to take its toll, however, leaving Jenni breathless. She decided to rest, choosing a stand of ancient pines. She breathed deeply of the fresh mountain air and knew a pleasure not possible anywhere else. The solitude and serenity of being one with God and at peace with her soul gave her the strength she needed to look for the answers that had eluded her.

Taking the pack from her back, Jenni found her well-worn Bible and began to pore over the Scriptures she'd come to love so dearly. Her eyes fell on verses nine and ten of Philippians chapter one: "And this is my prayer: that your love may abound more and more in knowledge and depth of insight, so that you may be able to discern what is best and may be pure and blameless until the day of Christ."

She felt almost as if the Apostle Paul were offering up a petition on behalf of her own concerns. She was always amazed how personalized the Scriptures became, just when she needed to feel an intimacy with God.

Setting the Bible aside, Jenni looked out across the valley. "Father, I'm ready to do whatever You direct me to do. Please let me be aware of Your guidance and help me to accept Your will as my own."

For a long time after that, she sat and watched the shadows fall across the valley floor. At noon, she took off her heavy sweater and rolled it up in order to squeeze it into the backpack. As she unzipped the pack, she noticed the candy kisses there.

"Oh, Dan," she murmured against the wind. "How can I love you so much and know nothing about you?" She listened to her own words, and then she said, her voice louder this time and filled with wonder, "I love him!"

The words hit her like a revelation. She had known their truth for some time, but only now could she deal with it. "I really love him," she admitted. "I can't imagine life without him and I don't know what I would do if I had to say goodbye to him now."

The wind picked up slightly and large puffy white clouds

blew over the jutted peaks. The sky was a rich hue of cobalt blue, and the cotton ball billows brought signs of a fall storm.

Jenni reached down to still the Bible pages that fluttered in the breeze. "I trust You, Father," Jenni murmured, making her way down the pathway.

The clouds turned from white to gray and then blackened, heavy with rain. Jenni had just made it to the car, when the first rain drops started to fall. She threw her pack across the front seat and headed to the ranger station. After checking in with the same attendant, Jenni headed out the south park gates and back to O'Reilly's.

She pulled into her usual place and parked. As she made her way into the office cabin, she was grateful to find a warm fire blazing in the hearth.

"Kelly, I'm back," Jenni called out as she picked up the mail on the office counter and began to sift through it.

"I was beginning to wonder where you were," Kelly said, coming through the back door. "I thought I might have to call out the troops."

"I'm sorry," Jenni apologized. "It was just so beautiful and I couldn't bear to leave. That is, until I saw those clouds move in."

Kelly shook off a few raindrops. "I know what you mean. I had to check in a last minute guest. I told him we were lucky to have any vacancies at all, but it just so happened that cabin six was empty so I put him there. He insisted that I bring him extra wood and towels, so I had to go over there in the rain."

"Some guests can be very inconsiderate."

"Oh, that's okay. By the way, he's from Topeka. Looked important too," Kelly said as she toweled dry her blond hair by the fire's warmth.

"Um," Jenni said in a rather disinterested way. "I'll have to check the register and see if the name rings a bell." She made no effort to go to the computer, though, feeling too tired to move.

"You look worn out. Why don't you go lay down for a while," Kelly suggested. "I'm fine now and I don't intend to go out again unless it's an emergency."

"I think you're right," Jenni yawned. "I'm beat."

She got up and crossed the room to the hallway. "By the way," Kelly called after her, "did you figure anything out?"

"As a matter of fact, I did," Jenni said simply. "I intend to sit down and talk to Dan tonight. If he won't give me any answers, then I'm going to end the relationship." The words seemed so effortless, and yet Jenni felt a stabbing pain inside her heart.

"That's quite a bit of figuring," Kelly replied. "Are you sure?"

"Yes," Jenni said reluctantly. "I have to put God first. No, I *want* to put God first and I can't do that if the man I love doesn't love God."

"So you love Dan?"

"Of course—but then you've always known that," Jenni said with a smile.

"Well, I'm just a good guesser," Kelly said with a shrug of her shoulders. "I've seen enough falling in love around me to know what it looks like. You know, 'always a bridesmaid, never a bride.'"

Jenni laughed at this. "My track record isn't exactly good, given the outcome of my previous relationship with Brian Givens."

At this, Kelly's face turned ashen, but she tried to hide her feelings from Jenni. "You'd better hurry. It's already two-thirty and I get to leave at five."

"Are you sure you're okay?" Jenni questioned. "You don't look well."

"I'm fine," Kelly assured. "Now go on, you're going to need your rest."

As soon as Jenni had closed her door, Kelly rushed to the computer and called up the information she'd just typed in before Jenni's return. She sat down hard, as the computer confirmed her fears.

Brian Givens was the guest she'd registered in cabin six.

"Dear Lord," she prayed, "please help us all."

eleven

Kelly was about to wake Jenni up when Dan walked through the office door. He smiled a hello at Kelly and asked her about Jenni.

"She's taking a nap. I was just about to wake her up," Kelly's words answered his question, but her face left a new concern in Dan's heart.

"Is she all right? You look upset about something." Dan spoke out of genuine concern. Kelly looked like she'd seen a ghost.

"I—uh—Jenni is fine, for now," Kelly began, wondering if she would be doing the right thing by telling Dan about Brian's arrival.

"For now?" Dan questioned. He moved closer to Kelly, who was avoiding his intense eyes. "What's going on, Kelly?"

Kelly picked at the buttons on her red gingham camp shirt. "I don't know if I should be telling you this or not," she said anxiously. "But that guy, Brian Givens—you know who I mean?" Dan nodded and Kelly continued, "He's here. He's just rented cabin six."

"Here? What for?" Dan hoped that Kelly would still the fear inside him that was growing stronger by the minute.

"I'm not sure. I mean, I think I know why he's here, but he didn't say anything if that's what you want to know."

Dan unzipped the leather bomber's jacket he wore and pushed his hands deep into the pockets of his blue jeans. "So," he started, "just what do you think you know about this, Kelly?"

"I don't know that I should tell you anymore, Dan. I just thought maybe you could. . ." her words fell silent.

"You thought I could what?"

"I thought you could tell Jenni. She doesn't know yet." Kelly looked troubled. "Please, Dan. I think she needs to know— and I hate to be the one to tell her. . ."

Dan grimaced and ran a hand through his thick hair. "I suppose you're right about telling her before she runs into him here. It might be more than a little awkward for her." Dan seemed to be reasoning aloud. "I'll tell her."

"I was just going to wake her up. I have to leave in a half hour or so, but I'll be here to cover the desk until then. In the meantime, why don't you wake her up for me? Then you two can have a private talk," Kelly suggested.

"All right," Dan agreed and took off his jacket. He made his way to Jenni's bedroom.

For a moment, Dan leaned against the doorway, watching Jenni as she slept. Her brown hair cascaded around her shoulders and spilled onto the pillow. Her thick lashes stayed closed tightly in sleep even when Dan came to sit on the bed beside her, leaving the door open behind him.

Pushing back a strand of hair, Dan couldn't help but wonder if Brian's appearance would put an end to his plans with Jennifer Campbell. He felt angry even thinking about coming face to face with the man who'd hurt Jenni so badly. Dan could think of quite a few things he'd like to say to the calloused and cold-hearted Brian Givens. Down deep inside, however, Dan knew that he would refrain from saying anything. Unless, of course, he was provoked.

"Jenni," he whispered her name softly. His hand stroked her cheek ever so lightly. "Wake up, Jenni."

Jenni opened her eyes to find Dan bent over her. She smiled. She had dreamt they were married. She had been Mrs. Daniel

James. Jennifer James. She had to admit, it had a nice ring to it. Now, here he was.

"Dan. What are you doing here?" she asked sleepily. She thought maybe she was still dreaming. When Dan pulled her into his arms and kissed her, Jenni knew, however, that it was no dream.

Suddenly conscious of the fact that she was in bed, she pushed him away. "You shouldn't be here."

"I'm sorry. Kelly asked me to wake you and. . ." he grinned broadly as Jenni blushed. "What can I say?" He shrugged his shoulders as he spoke.

Jenni laughed, but in her heart she was aware of her earlier decision to talk to Dan about God. The memory dampened her spirits, and noticing this, Dan pulled her close again.

He grimaced over Jenni's head. He hated to spoil their time together by bringing up the bad news that Brian Givens was in town.

Jenni placed her head against Dan's broad chest and sighed. How very nice it would be if she could only do this every time she woke up.

"Dan. . ."

"Jenni. . ."

Both of them started to speak at the same time. Jenni couldn't help but laugh at the serious look on Dan's face. He was so seldom serious, that Jenni thought perhaps he was just uncomfortable about being in her bedroom.

"You go ahead," Jenni prompted.

"No, you," Dan insisted. "What I have to say isn't all that pleasant."

Jenni's look of alarm matched the concern in her voice. "What's wrong? Is it Kelly?"

"No, no. Kelly is fine," Dan hushed. He saw the fear in her eyes and his helplessness to change the situation overwhelmed him. He wanted to hug her to him, but instead he drew back a little. "Please don't look like that."

"Like what?" she questioned in concern.

"Like a lost child. So big-eyed and scared," Dan said in a husky whisper. He reached his hand to Jenni's face and cupped her chin in it. "Don't be afraid. I won't let anything or anybody hurt you."

Jenni felt comforted by his words, but nonetheless she felt a nagging worry that something was terribly wrong, something that would change things between herself and Dan.

"Anybody?" Jenni questioned warily. "What are you talking about? Tell me now."

Dan pushed back his hair, and lowered his face. When he raised it again to look deep into Jenni's eyes, he had managed to steady his nerves. "Brian Givens is in Estes," he said matter-of-factly.

"What!" Jenni exclaimed. "Brian? Here?"

"I'm sorry, Jenni. Kelly asked me to tell you. She knew it wouldn't be pleasant news," Dan offered sympathetically.

"But how does she know? She doesn't know Brian or what he looks like. How does she know he's here?" But even as Jenni said the words, she began to remember her earlier conversation with Kelly. Before Dan could answer, Jenni continued, "Kelly said she'd checked someone new into cabin six. Someone from Topeka who acted like he was important. Brian is here at O'Reilly's, isn't he?"

"Yes," Dan affirmed softly.

Jenni buried her face in her hands. "Oh, no! Why is this happening?"

"It's all right, Jenni. Everything will work out for good, you'll see," Dan tried to assure her, but despite the fact that his words came very close to one of her favorite Bible verses, Jenni was not comforted.

"Oh, Dan, I don't want him here. I don't want to see him. Everything was finally beginning to make sense again. I hadn't thought of Brian in weeks." As she spoke, she felt almost as if Dan were just another of her friends, instead of the man she'd given serious thoughts to spending the rest of her life with. "I'm not going to stay here while he's here. I'll move."

"You're the manager here. Did you forget that?" Dan questioned, as he stroked Jenni's hair.

Jenni heaved a sigh. "Yes, I did." Throwing her head back, Jenni stared for a moment at the ceiling. "I'm afraid of seeing him, Dan." She had nothing to lose by being honest.

"I know," Dan said softly as she slowly lowered her gaze to meet his eyes.

"You know? How could you know what I'm feeling?" Jenni questioned with a whisper.

"I've been there. Just because I'm not married or divorced, doesn't mean I haven't had my heart broken. I'm a seasoned veteran, believe me."

"Does it get any better?" Jenni wondered aloud.

"Yes, it does. Especially if you have something else to interest yourself with," Dan said simply.

"Something, or someone?" Jenni tried to tease.

"Either way, it gets your heart on the mend and your mind off the past." His eyes were intensely blue and Jenni felt herself falling in love, all over again. The kindness, the soft boyishness of his face, his gentle tone, all these things made her love Dan James with all her heart.

"Oh, Dan," Jenni whispered, letting him embrace her again. Her mind was engulfed with the fearful wonder of why Brian had come to Estes.

"I must say, you certainly aren't the frigid ice queen I left in Topeka," Brian's sarcastic voice rang out.

Jenni pulled away from Dan, suddenly conscious of how

this encounter must look to Brian. Dan stood up, but made no offer to move away from Jenni. Jenni sat opened-mouthed, staring at Brian. She was completely unable to speak.

"I didn't expect to see you," she managed to say, finally finding her voice.

"I can see that," Brian smirked.

"If you can't speak respectfully to this woman, then don't waste her time," Dan said in a menacing tone Jenni had never heard him use before.

"Ah, the new man on the block," Brian said with a superior air. "Did she tell you that she has a fiance?"

"Had," Jenni stated flatly. "Had a fiance. Why are you here, Brian?" The irritation was clear in her voice.

"I came for you." He spoke as if Dan were nothing more than another piece of furniture.

Jennifer couldn't keep from gasping aloud. "You have to be joking." She threw back the covers so that he would see she was fully dressed.

"I'm completely serious. By the way, who's your friend?" Brian sneered.

Dan stood eye to eye with Brian. The tension was unbearable. "The name is James. Daniel James," Dan said, moving forward to edge Brian out of the room.

Jennifer grew more uncomfortable. She prayed silently that neither man would resort to using force. For several minutes nobody said a word. She finally realized that she had to end the stalemate. "Please leave, Brian. I have nothing to say to you and I don't want to see you." Her words were surprisingly calm.

"You heard her," Dan added. "Now do I have to force you?"

"I seriously doubt that you could," Brian said, giving Daniel a brief look. "But, under the circumstances, I'll go. But," he added with his gaze fixed firmly on Jennifer, "only as far as the living room. We're going to talk."

"Very well," Jenni said sternly. "If you'll both wait outside, I'll be there directly."

Daniel's eyes never left Brian as they moved from the room. Closing the door behind them, Jenni sank to the floor. "Dear God," she began to sob, "make it all go away."

Nearly twenty minutes had passed before Jenni joined the two stern-faced men in her living room. Her eyes were red-rimmed, and both Dan and Brian knew that she'd been crying.

Dan couldn't help but wonder if seeing Brian had caused Jenni's old feelings to return. He shoved his hands deep into his jeans and leaned against the stone wall beside the fireplace.

Brian, on the other hand, started to move toward Jennifer. "Stay back," Jenni said raising her hand. "I don't want you to touch me and I don't want you crowding me."

Brian looked surprised, but he stayed where he was. Dan knew better than to say a word and remained fixed to the wall.

Jenni moved past both of them and went to where the coffee was warming for the resort guests. She poured herself a cup, hoping it would steady her nerves.

She stood for a moment looking first at Dan and then at Brian. Neither one said a word, and Jenni's face remained blank. Dan wished he knew her better in order to read her thoughts.

With an unsettling calm, Jenni took a seat on the rock ledge on the opposite side of the fireplace from where Dan stood. "Brian," she finally spoke in a barely audible voice, "I don't want to hurt your feelings, but I really have nothing to say to you. When I think about you, about us, I only feel sad. Not because it's over, but because of all the time I wasted with you."

Brian opened his mouth, but Jenni put out her hand. "No, don't say anything. I want you to hear me for once. You're so used to running the show. You always called the shots in our relationship and I think it's about time you considered someone else beside yourself."

"You're right, of course," Brian said ignoring her request for silence.

Jenni was surprised at his agreeable comment, but Dan remained unimpressed. He crossed his arms against his chest and narrowed his eyes as he examined Brian Givens closely.

"Can't we talk alone?" Brian asked Jenni earnestly.

"No," Jenni answered quickly. "I don't trust you and I haven't any desire to be alone with you."

Brian tried to hide his rage with a look of disappointment. "All those years mean nothing to you?" he questioned sadly.

"I didn't say that," Jenni replied. "They mean a great deal. They taught me about deception and pain. I've learned well to gauge my future relationships by the mistakes I've made in the past. Especially," she said pausing to glance at Dan before returning her gaze to Brian, "in regards to being unequally yoked with unbelievers."

"But, Jenni," Brian's voice took on a pleading tone, "the things that separated us, that made me say and do the things I did, no longer exist. Things have changed. I've changed."

"I don't care." Jenni responded.

Dan was almost enjoying Brian's discomfort. If he didn't feel compassion for most troubled souls, he'd have laughed out loud. Even so, for Jennifer's sake, he'd do nothing more than observe.

"Jennifer, you don't understand," Brian tried to explain, but Jenni cut him off.

"That's right, Brian. I don't understand." She began to realize that this was an opportunity to share many of her feelings regarding God and Christianity, with both Brian and Dan. She wasn't about to miss her chance. "I don't understand how a person could make money or power his god, and forsake the Savior that was sent to die for him, so long ago. I realize that when I do marry, if I marry, it will be to a man who has accepted salvation in Jesus. A man who has turned his whole heart towards God's will and seeks to live by the Bible. A true man of God."

Brian got up and walked to the living room window. He gazed out across the mountain range and the purple-hued sky. Twilight had left pink streaks against the dusky tones of evening. With tears in his eyes, Brian turned back to face Jennifer and Dan.

"But that's what I've been trying to tell you, Jenni. I have accepted Christ. I realized you were right. Your words to me, all the words you spoke about God over and over, they finally hit home. I realized once you'd gone that I was really alone. I thought breaking up with you would dispel the frustration and anguish I felt inside, but God had other plans. You were right, Jenni, and I knew I had to deal with my spiritual battle. I made peace with God and that's why I'm here. I had to tell you and win you back."

twelve

Dan had remained silent long enough. Pushing away from the wall, he came to stand between Jenni and Brian.

"Even if you have accepted the truth of salvation, what makes you think you have the right to come in here, insult Jenni, and then tell her in practically the same breath that you want to win her back?"

Jenni was captivated by his statement about accepting the truth of salvation. Could it be that Dan knew the truth? Momentarily, Jenni lost track of the words exchanged by Brian and Daniel. The world seemed so crazy right now.

"I can't believe you have the nerve to even show your face, Givens," Dan said quietly to the still seated Brian.

At this, Brian got quickly to his feet and stood within inches of Dan's face. "Just who do you think you are? I was engaged to this woman for two years and knew her long before that!" Brian exclaimed.

"*Was* is the important word here," Dan returned coolly. "The word is past tense, if you notice. It implies a condition that no longer exists."

Jenni watched them as if they were actors in a play. The two men continued to argue even as she got to her feet and made her way outside. She could hear them from the balcony, and as she gazed into the darkening sky, she found herself praying for guidance.

"So that's why you acted as if she were behaving indecently with me?" Dan was questioning Brian now. Jenni couldn't stand anymore and left the balcony by way of the outside stairs.

She knew it was foolhardy in the dim light of late evening, but nevertheless she climbed up the mountainside toward the sanctuary of the solitary peaks far above. After climbing several hundred feet, she took a seat on top of a boulder and gazed back down on O'Reilly's and the Fall River Canyon. The scene was so deceptively peaceful. How could the rest of the world not know about the battle that raged below her?

Oblivious to the cold, she sat for over an hour. At one point, she heard Brian and Dan calling her name, but she refused to answer. She could not deal with this situation. What was she supposed to do?

Stars like crystals shed their light in the black night sky. The cold was penetrating Jenni's bones now, causing her to tremble from the lack of warmth. Still, she didn't want to go home.

Home? Funny how she'd come so soon to consider O'Reilly's home. She seldom thought of Topeka or of anything there.

"I thought I'd find you up here," Dan's voice sounded.

Jenni was startled, but not unhappy with his appearance. "I couldn't take it," she admitted. She was shivering uncontrollably and her teeth were chattering.

"Come on. You can stay in my cabin until you warm up and we can talk," Dan said as he took hold of Jenni's arm. She allowed him to lead her back to his cabin. The cold numbing her brain made her unable to think clearly, but she noticed that despite the cool air, Dan was careful to leave the front door open. From outside, the voices of other visitors to O'Reilly's were clearly audible, dispelling the sense of intimacy that she might otherwise have felt alone with Dan in his cabin.

Sitting in front of Dan's fireplace with a blanket wrapped

around her and a cup of hot chocolate in her hand, Jenni's mind began to resurface until once again she could think rationally.

"I'm sorry about arguing with your Mr. Givens," Dan started.

"He's not my anything," Jenni corrected.

Dan grinned and his eyes betrayed his satisfaction with her answer. "Good. I'm glad to hear it."

"Oh, Dan, why did this have to happen? I don't want to have to deal with this," Jenni said as she gazed into the fire. "It just isn't fair. I was just starting to figure out what I wanted, and then this."

"Does Brian really change anything?" Dan questioned as he came to sit beside Jenni on the couch.

"In some senses, no. In others, I'm not so sure," Jenni answered honestly.

"Such as?"

"Such as," Jenni hesitated. "Such as the issue of God and salvation."

"I see," Dan said distantly as he sat to the edge of the seat. He refused to look at Jenni, but she could tell his mind and soul were troubled.

"What is this all about, Dan? Every time I bring up God, you seem further and further away. Is it that hard to conceive that this issue would have to be cleared between us before we could go on with a relationship of any serious degree?" Jenni finally felt bold enough to lay all her cards on the table.

"No, I know it's important. I just feel that now is the worst possible timing. I have that writers' conference coming up in less than a week," Dan replied in a subdued tone.

"And what does the writers' conference have to do with this issue?" Jenni asked, puzzled by Dan's reference to the conference. She suddenly realized that she hadn't even thought to find out whether he'd decided to accept the speaking request or not.

Dan walked to the fireplace and carefully placed another log on the fire. The silence stretched into minutes, but Jenni was determined to wait as long as was needed to get her answer.

Dan stood up and walked back to the couch. For a moment all he could do was stare intently at Jenni's face. Would she understand, he wondered. Would she believe the words he needed to say?

Jenni placed the empty cup on the coffee table and patted the seat beside her. "I'm waiting," she announced seriously. "I need answers, Dan."

The color seemed to drain from Dan's face. He looked at Jenni and then to the notebook computer that sat on his dining room table. "I have obligations, Jenni. Things that I can't explain. I want you to believe me when I say that I wish I could give you the assurance you need, but I can't. I need to work through some things and I don't know when I can feel free to explain."

Jenni tried to weigh the answer in light of all that had happened. She tried her best to be fair about her decision, but she knew Dan wouldn't be pleased with the outcome.

"I made a decision today," she began, "while I was hiking in Rocky Mountain National Park." She shrugged off the blanket, and got to her feet. "I decided that if we couldn't come to terms on the issues of God and salvation, I would have to end this courtship."

Dan's face fell. The hurt in his eyes, the look of desolation, nearly made Jenni lose her resolve. She walked to the door, however, certain that God wouldn't want her to even think about a serious relationship with a man who hadn't accepted Christ as his Savior.

"It's Brian, isn't it?" Dan accused. "You want to end this courtship so you can pick up with him again." He was angry now, and grasping at straws.

"How could you even think such a thing?" Jenni gasped. "You know how he's hurt me. You know what I went through. I don't trust Brian Givens and I'm not sure he's telling the truth about accepting Christ. Even if he is, I don't think I could ever love him again after he hurt me so badly. But I don't know what to believe about you. So I'm stuck in the middle."

"I can't believe that after all this time, you still question my intentions."

"It isn't your intentions that worry me," Jenni said sadly. "It's your lack of understanding or even interest in why Christianity is important to me—and why the man I marry needs to be a Christian."

Dan came to Jenni and took her in his arms. She stiffly complied with his embrace, but her heart felt distant from him. "Please, Jenni, just give me some time. I can't explain yet, but trust me. Please."

"I can't court you, not with the serious values you placed on courtship," she said. His grief-stricken face, though, made her soften her decision. "I will, however, date you. But, I will also date others and our relationship will not be exclusive."

Without waiting for his reply, she broke free from his embrace and walked out the door.

When she returned to the office cabin, Jenni warily glanced around, half expecting Brian to still be there. When she found the cabin empty she heaved a sigh of relief.

❧

Most of the night, Jenni tossed and turned. Her sleep was fitful at best and when the office phone rang first thing in the morning, Jenni dragged herself out of bed to answer it.

"O'Reilly's, Jennifer Campbell speaking." She knew she sounded groggy, but glancing at her watch it was no wonder. It was only seven o-clock in the morning.

"Jen, it's Brian, please don't hang up."

Jenni was instantly awake. "What do you want?" Her heart pounded suddenly. She was almost afraid.

"I've got to talk to you, but not with James there. I want to speak to you alone. I've got to talk to you and I don't have that long to be out here. You know the election is in less than three weeks."

"Yes, I know," Jenni said ignoring his desperation. "I can't imagine why you left your duties in Topeka to come here."

"I wanted you back in my life. Jenni, you're the best thing that ever happened to me. I was a complete fool to lose you. I can't live without you, you have to believe me."

"I don't believe you, Brian, but probably not for the reasons you think. While it did take a long time to get over the hurt, it didn't take long at all to realize it was the right decision. We don't belong together, Brian. Our priorities are just not the same in life," Jenni answered firmly.

"But they are now. God is important to me too. I realize I took an awful long time in figuring that out, but, Jenni, I need you. I can't go home without you by my side," Brian said desperately.

"Look, I have no intention of returning to Topeka just yet. I promised my folks I'd come home for election night, but that's all. I like Estes Park and I plan to stay here," she said, realizing that she meant every word. She had decided to live in Estes permanently.

"You can't be serious," Brian tried to persuade. "Think of all you have back home. Think of your parents. Why, they've been heartsick ever since you've been in Colorado. I know, because I see them all the time."

"Brian, you're just trying to change my mind and it won't work. I've already discussed this with my folks and they thought the idea was a good one," Jenni replied.

"Of course they'd say that," Brian remarked. "They don't want you to feel bad about your choice. But I can tell you, Jen, they aren't the same people since you left."

Jenni felt a twinge of fear that perhaps Brian's words were true. Maybe her parents really were heartsick and maybe they were hiding their true feelings from her. Brian apparently recognized the pause in the conversation as an affirmation that his words had hit home.

"You really should consider what's going on back home before you make plans to live here. After all, you don't really belong here," he pressed.

Jenni had listened to all she could tolerate. "Brian, I'm tired, and I'm going back to bed. I will talk to you more later but—"

"When?" Brian interrupted.

"I don't know," Jenni replied, the irritation in her voice beginning to show.

"Have lunch with me," Brian begged. "Please. Just lunch downtown, you can even meet me there if you don't trust me to drive you." When she said nothing, Brian continued. "Come on, Jen. Just to talk. Even if you don't love me anymore, you can at least just listen to me. I've come all this way, after all."

Jenni could no longer stand the pleading. "All right, lunch. But that's it. I'll meet you downtown at Poppy's, at twelve-thirty, but until then," she said, then paused for a second, "just leave me alone."

thirteen

Jenni followed Highway 34 into Estes, but her mind was a million miles away from the river road she travelled. Why had Brian come back into her life?

"Father," she found herself praying, "what is the purpose in this? I thought I put the past aside—and now You bring Brian back into it. I just don't understand."

A light rain started to fall, clouding the valley below in a misty, gossamer veil. The rain gradually built until a sizeable downpour was threatening Jenni's visibility. "Lord," she whispered, "I know that Psalm 121 says You will keep me from all harm and that You will watch over my life. I need that right now." As she remembered the rest of the verse, she experienced a sudden revelation that her prayer didn't rise only out of concern for the road's hazardous condition. Softly, she said the words of the verse out loud: "the Lord will watch over your coming and going both now and forevermore."

Glancing in her rear view mirror, she saw a sudden patch of blue appear in the skies behind her. The sun poured through that one spot, shooting rays of light in a fan across the sky. She remembered her sister Julie had once seen something similar and told her mother it was just like a little bit of heaven coming down.

"Thank you, Father God," Jenni breathed. "It *is* like a little bit of heaven coming down."

Her resolve strengthened as she found a place to park. She steadied her nerves, but in spite of the fact that the rain was gradually letting up, she found herself hesitant to get out of the car. "Give me strength, Lord," she whispered.

When the rain was little more than a sprinkle, Jenni got out of her car and headed into Poppy's. Brian was already there, waiting and watching her as she entered.

He wore a white fisherman's sweater and olive green corduroy pants, clothes more casual than Jenni could ever remember him being willing to wear before. He smiled when he saw Jenni and got up from the booth to accompany her to their table.

"I'm glad you came." He possessively took hold of her arm. Jenni pulled away so abruptly that she almost lost her balance. Brian frowned slightly but said nothing.

"I hope it's all right, but I've already ordered for us," he said, taking the seat opposite Jennifer in the booth.

"I don't care either way," she said rather stiffly.

"Well, I didn't want to overstep my boundaries, but I was hungry. I ordered a sausage pizza with everything. It ought to be here anytime."

Just then a waitress appeared with the pizza and asked Jenni for her drink order. "I'll have iced tea with lemon," Jenni replied. Brian, Jenni noticed, was drinking his customary black coffee.

Jenni hadn't planned to eat, but suddenly she felt very hungry. She offered to say grace for both of them, and when Brian quickly agreed, she had to bite her tongue to keep from commenting on the rarity of the moment. Public prayer was always an embarrassment to Brian in the past. Jenni offered a short, but heartfelt prayer. As she whispered, "Amen," she looked up to find Brian already at work on the pizza.

For several moments they did nothing more than share a meal. Jenni felt strange being so uncomfortable with the man she'd once planned to spend the rest of her life with. She couldn't help but notice the harshness in his face and eyes.

Maybe it was just her imagination, but Jenni was certain that given time, she'd have her answers as to the reality of Brian's conversion.

After devouring three large slices of pizza, Brian leaned back in the booth and watched Jenni as she worked on her second piece. "The mountain air has obviously been good for you. You look great," he finally said.

Jenni put her food down and tried to think of a reply. She was still mulling over what to say, when Brian continued. "I've really missed you, Jen," he whispered.

"I didn't think much about you at all," Jenni said honestly. She knew the words were caustic, but she felt she needed to say the truth. "I just wanted to forget everything about us." She emphasized the word "us."

Brian looked rather taken aback, but he was still soft-spoken when he said, "I guess I deserved that. You have a right to be upset with me. I wasn't very good to you and I hope that you'll forgive me."

Jenni let out a sigh and rolled her eyes heavenward. She was faced with a dilemma. He sought her forgiveness, he said, and not to give it would be to betray all of the things she believed. Why was this happening? If she forgave him, she would be forced to face up to the past and the hurt.

"I know I don't deserve to be forgiven," Brian said as if reading Jenni's mind. "But, it is important to me. I felt that even if I couldn't win you back, I had to have your forgiveness."

Jenni found herself holding her breath. Why did he have to be saying all the correct and proper things? Letting out a long sigh, she finally spoke. "I do forgive you, Brian." She sighed, realizing she had spoken the truth. "But I don't want anything more to do with you. I've put that part of my life aside and now I'm interested in other things."

"Like Daniel James?" Brian asked in a snide manner.

"Not that it's your concern, but yes. I've seen quite a bit of Dan this summer and I have come to truly enjoy his company," Jenni answered.

"Isn't that a bit of a rebound romance? You haven't even been away from me for more than a few months."

"Actually, I began seeing Dan after only a few weeks," Jenni couldn't help but add in her own sarcastic tone. "I couldn't see prolonging the mourning period. After all, I came to the conclusion that you had done me a big favor. Our priorities were so different that I couldn't see any hope of planning the same goals or dreams."

"And you can with this James character?" Brian questioned as he leaned across the table. "He doesn't know you like I do, Jen. He never will."

Jenni narrowed her eyes slightly, and frowned. "I didn't come here to discuss Dan James with you. I came here with only one purpose in mind and that was to tell you I wanted nothing more to do with you."

"Are you really sure?" Brian questioned. Noticing a change in Jenni's expression, he took new hope. "See, I knew that there was more to this than a simple ending. The look on your face says that I'm right."

Jenni shook her head. "No, the look on my face is not a signal to you that I want to get back together."

"Oh, I get it," Brian said, leaning back and crossing his arms across his chest. "You want me to beg. I've hurt you, so now you want to hurt me and make me pay."

Jenni nearly laughed out loud and would have if the situation had not been so pathetic. "You couldn't be any further from the truth. Brian, I did a lot of thinking right after you walked out of my life. I questioned God, looked for answers, and eventually made my peace. I realize now that you have a destructive nature about you that I cannot tolerate. You go after things and destroy whatever stands in your way. You care little for human life, or the feelings surrounding those lives."

"You forget one thing," Brian interrupted. "That was before I got religion."

"Got religion? You say it as if it were a credit card you'd applied for. Which brings me around to the second part of what I wanted to say and that is, I really don't know that I can believe what you say regarding your salvation. It isn't my place to judge your sincerity—but one thing I know and that is this—your actions will speak for themselves."

"And how will you know of those actions, if you refuse to see me? All I want is a chance to prove myself," Brian said sadly.

Jenni supposed he was right, but inside, her mind was warning her away. "What is it you expect from me?"

"I'm going to be here until the end of the month. Then I have to get back and help with the two campaigns I'm involved in. During my stay here, I want you to go out with me."

"Oh, please," Jenni said in an exasperated tone, "why can't you just leave me out of it?"

"Because I love you, Jenni, and I still want to marry you."

Brian's simple words pierced Jenni's heart. All she could think about was the tear-filled nights she'd spent after Brian's break-up with her.

"I don't know what to say," she finally whispered.

"Just say that you'll at least think about it," Brian begged. "Please!"

The urgency in his voice and the pleading in his eyes was too much. Jenni got up quickly and ran from the room.

Out on the street, she didn't stop running until she was safe in her car. How could he do this to her? How could she possibly bear to reopen that painful relationship?

She drove for hours, and only when she realized that the sun was going down, did she make her way back to O'Reilly's. As she pulled into her parking place, Kelly came running from the cabin.

"Where have you been? Dan and I have been so worried," Kelly was saying as Jenni got out of the car.

"Oh, Kelly, please tell me that Dan isn't here," Jenni pleaded.

"No, he's up at his cabin. But I have to let him know you got back okay. He's been beside himself." Kelly replied. "Don't you want him to know that you're safe?"

"Of course, but—" Jenni broke into a fresh onslaught of tears.

"Come on," Kelly said as she pulled Jenni along. "You go take a hot shower, and I'll go tell Dan that you're safe but indisposed."

"I just can't take this pressure," Jenni cried.

"What did Brian do to put you in this frame of mind?" Kelly couldn't help questioning.

"He wants me to date him while he's here in Estes. Oh, Kelly, he says he still loves me and wants to marry me!"

"And what do you feel about him?"

"I don't want to even explore the possibility. I can't bear to think of Brian and the past. I was just trying to settle things with Dan. I broke off the courtship because he won't level with me about his spiritual convictions. I'm so confused and I just don't know what to do anymore."

"Then you need to rest, pray, and get into the Word," Kelly said as she guided Jenni to her bedroom. "Now, look, you get a shower and settle down in bed and I'll bring you some supper."

"No, Kelly," Jenni said shaking her head. "I think I'm going to need more than just the regular prayer session this time. No food. And Kelly?"

"What?"

"I'm going to lock this door and not come out until I feel better about things. Can you handle the resort?" Jenni felt it was too much to ask, but she had no other choice.

"Of course. Don't give it another thought," Kelly moved to the door. "By the way," she added. "I'll be praying too."

"Thanks, Kelly. You couldn't be a better friend."

Later, after Jenni had carefully shampooed her hair and showered, she got into her bed with the Bible.

ॐ

From the top of the hillside, not more than a stone's throw from his cabin, Dan stood in the cold night air. He stared down at the light that still shone from Jenni's room.

It was three in the morning. "Can she still be praying and reading?" he wondered silently.

He'd been so relieved when Kelly had come to the cabin to tell him that Jenni had returned. He hadn't felt right since she'd left his cabin the night before, but with Brian Givens pressuring her into meeting him, Dan felt even more frustration.

He studied the cabin below him for a while longer, then finally succumbed to the cold and went inside. He undressed for bed and then, without a second thought, Dan James fell to his knees and began to pray.

fourteen

Jenni emerged from her haven nearly sixteen hours later. Kelly's eyes held dark circles under them, betraying that she too had slept very little during Jenni's ordeal.

"Well?" Kelly asked cautiously.

Jenni drew a deep breath, "I read in Titus one, verses fifteen and sixteen, 'To the pure, all things are pure, but to those who are corrupted and do not believe, nothing is pure. In fact, both their minds and consciences are corrupted. They claim to know God, but by their actions they deny him. They are detestable, disobedient and unfit for doing anything good.'"

"And?" Kelly pressed.

"And I feel God has used this verse to show me something. Daniel wants me to trust him, telling me that he'll explain everything later. Brian tells me everything, explaining that he'll show me as time goes on. Their actions will prove their hearts, Kelly."

Kelly nodded. "That seems reasonable, but will Dan see it that way?"

"Why do you question whether Dan will see it that way?" Jenni asked. "What about Brian?"

"Brian already knows he has competition. Dan doesn't," Kelly replied.

"But I've already broken the courtship with Dan. I told him that I would see him, but I would also see other people. I just didn't expect one of those people to be Brian," Jenni stated.

"Jenni, do you still care for Brian?"

Jenni shook her head. "No, but I feel that I owe it to him to let him prove himself."

"You feel you owe it to him? After what he did to you, how could you think you owe him anything?" Kelly asked, straining to control her disbelief.

"I must live by the principles set for me in the Bible, Kelly. It doesn't mean that I'll marry Brian, it just means that I'll allow him to show me that he's truly changed. By the first of November," Jenni concluded, "I should be able to figure out who is telling the truth."

⋟

After a week of sharing time between Dan and Brian, Jenni was beginning to dread seeing either one of them come down the path toward the office.

"I'm tired of this, Kelly," Jenni began one evening as she waited for Brian to arrive. He was taking her to the symphony in Denver. "I don't know why I agreed to go all the way to Denver with Brian."

"Just relax, Jenni," Kelly smiled. "It won't be much longer until the first of November."

"I could be completely insane by then," Jenni said, waiting for her escort. "Tonight is a good example. Two hours to Denver, two hours at the concert, and then another two hours back. Not to mention that somewhere in there I'm sure Brian will want to stop for dinner."

"You sound like you're really dreading it," Kelly sympathized.

"It's going to be well past midnight before we get back," Jenni said with a sigh.

"Maybe it's more than that," Kelly suggested.

"Maybe," Jenni said absentmindedly. The fact was, Kelly was right. Jenni was getting the distinct impression that Brian was getting too serious about their relationship.

"Has Brian been pushing you too hard?" Kelly questioned,

seeming to read Jenni's mind.

"I just have a feeling," Jenni said, getting to her feet. "I can't really put my finger on it, but I guess I'm almost afraid."

"Has Brian done something to frighten you?" Kelly's concern was clear.

"No, not like you mean. He's been a perfect gentleman, but there's something about him. I know he's just a new Christian and all, but he seems so uncomfortable when I suggest we pray or when I want to share something from Scripture with him."

"Have you asked Brian why he decided after all this time to accept Christ?" Kelly questioned.

"No, not really. I haven't exactly had time. When I'm with Brian he talks ninety miles an hour. I seldom have a chance to bring up anything and when I try to change the subject, he accuses me of being evasive," Jenni replied.

Just then the doorbell rang, and Brian entered the room, resplendent in his evening wear. His black tuxedo stood out in sharp contrast to Jenni's cream colored evening gown. "You look magnificent, Jen," Brian offered and motioned her to turn around. "I want to see all of it," he said as he waved his hand and Jenni obediently turned.

The princess style cut of the velvet gown clung to her small frame as, the dressmaker had assured Jenni, good velvet should. The off-shoulder, draped neckline was trimmed with tiny seed pearls and sequins. Kelly had helped Jenni to put up her hair in a stylish sweep, with curls cascading down the back.

Brian smiled appreciatively. "What a couple we'll make tonight!"

"Well, Cinderella, just don't lose your slipper on the castle steps," Kelly laughed.

"If she should, her prince will be right behind her," Brian

said with a deep bow at the waist.

Kelly could see what Jenni had once found appealing in the dashing smile and suave grace of the dark-haired Brian. He was a definite charmer.

Despite Jenni's trepidation about the evening, she found herself actually enjoying Brian's companionship. She thought several times of Dan and tried to imagine the same evening with him, but she never lingered on the thoughts. They were almost painful to her.

"You're awfully quiet," Brian said as he maneuvered his rental car onto Highway 36 for the return trip to Estes.

"I'm just tired," Jenni replied. She spoke the truth, although perhaps her silence was caused by more than tiredness alone.

"I really enjoyed being with you tonight," Brian began again. "I think we work well together. Don't you?"

"You make dating sound like a business adventure or a law partnership," Jenni said rather distantly. She gazed out into the darkness past her window; except for an occasional lighted house, the rest of the world seemed to be asleep.

"I'm sorry. Sometimes I don't say the perfect or most romantic thing. I don't have Mr. James' penchant for words." Brian's voice took on a slightly sarcastic tone.

"This has nothing to do with Dan," Jenni said defensively. "You've always made relationships sound like business deals. I wonder if that will ever change."

"I won't stop being ambitious, if that's what you mean. I still want to achieve a great deal while I'm young, and then when I'm older I'll be set up to walk into whatever I choose." Brian spoke with pride.

"What about God's plan for your life, Brian?" Jenni questioned.

"God's plan is my plan," Brian said simply. "I wouldn't have it any other way. I'll just continue until God sends me word that I'm to do otherwise."

"I see," Jenni said softly. "And are you really open to change? If, indeed, God sends you word?"

"What's with all this questioning?" Brian was the one now whose voice was defensive. "I think I've proven myself. Or is there still some other test you're waiting for me to perform?"

"I don't understand," Jenni said, confused by Brian's mood.

Brian pulled the car off the highway and turned off the engine. "Come here, Jennifer."

"Why?" Jenni questioned suspiciously.

"Because I want to hold you. I haven't held you since the night before I left you. I've wanted to, at least a thousand times, and when I saw you tonight I wanted to take you in my arms then and there."

"I'm not sure that it would be wise." Jenni spoke more harshly than she'd intended.

"You'll share a bed with James, but you won't even let me hold you?" Brian retorted angrily.

"I've never shared a bed with anyone! How dare you accuse me? You know how I feel about saving myself for marriage. You above all others know that fact very well," Jenni replied, her temper barely in check.

"I'm sorry, Jen. I had to find out and I just didn't know a tactful way to ask. I thought maybe your values were different now. Passion does strange things to a person," Brian whispered softly.

Jenni tried to calm her shattered nerves and rethink Brian's request. Finally, she slid across the seat and allowed Brian to put his arms around her. He pulled her close in a rough embrace.

His touch wasn't like Dan's. Dan was more muscular, more sure of himself, yet gentle. The most exercise Brian got was during his racquetball games, and he'd never had a talent for treating Jenni gently.

She found herself suddenly aware of past feelings. Feelings of fear, danger, and dread, she realized, had always nagged at her whenever Brian had embraced her. If Brian decided to take advantage of her, she would be able to do very little to stop him.

"Kiss me, Jenni," Brian was whispering against her ear.

"No," Jenni said, trying to push him away.

"Just a kiss," he said and pulled her face roughly to his own. His roughness only caused Jenni to tense more. He lowered his lips to hers in an impassioned kiss, which Jenni fought.

She could feel his hands pushing at the velvet neckline, and though he held her pinned against the seat in a steely grip, she fought his advances. Finally freeing her mouth from his, she screamed, "Leave me alone! You haven't changed at all."

She expected to have to fight him more, but instead he released Jenni and put his face in his hands. "I'm so sorry, Jenni. So sorry."

Jenni moved to the far side of the car, one hand on the door handle in case she needed to get out. "Take me home," she whispered.

"I know I don't deserve your forgiveness, but please, Jenni, try to understand. You just look so beautiful, and I can't help wanting you. You have to know that I'm telling the truth. A new convert can't change overnight, but I'm trying to do my best," Brian said as he raised his eyes to meet Jenni's. "Please help me to do what's right."

Jenni's heart softened at his pleading. "It's all right. I understand, and I'm not angry. You're quite right. It is hard to change your worldly ways for divine ones, but Jesus will help you, Brian. He'll be better at it than me."

"I'm sure you're right, Jen. You won't let this hurt our

friendship, will you?" Brian said with such a pained expression that Jenni couldn't help but feel sorry for him.

"No, of course not. But it is late, Brian. I think we should get started again."

"Of course. And Jenni," Brian reached across the distance between them, "thank you, for forgiving me."

Jenni smiled, but said nothing. The remainder of the trip passed in silence, and she was relieved to see O'Reilly's sign come into sight.

Brian pulled up the inclined drive and stopped to let her out at the office cabin. He started to get out of the car, but she waved him off. "No, I'll be fine. Let's just say goodnight, and I'll see you tomorrow." Brian looked hurt, but reluctantly he agreed.

Jenni had barely had time to get inside when a soft knocking sounded at the office door. Dread filled her from head to toe. She moved to see who it was and was surprised to find Dan on the doorstep.

"Look, I know it's late, but we've got to talk," Dan said urgently.

Jenni had never seen such a look of worry and turmoil on anyone's face before. He seemed to be literally in pain from whatever dilemma haunted his mind.

"Sure," she finally answered. "Come on in."

"Is Kelly here? I mean, I need to talk to you about a very private matter," Dan said, looking toward the living room of the cabin.

"She's sound asleep, I'm sure," Jenni said, looking at her watch.

Dan seemed on the verge of breaking down. His face was haggard, and his coat did little to hide the wrinkled appearance of clothes that looked as though he had slept in them.

"Come on," Jenni said softly, leading him to the couch.

As if noticing her attire for the first time, Dan reached up his hand and gently traced the draped velvet across her shoulder. "You're beautiful. I hope Givens appreciated you tonight," Dan whispered.

"I don't wish to discuss Brian's appreciation," Jenni said in a way that caused Dan to frown.

"Did he act out of place with you?"

"Yes, you might say that. But I took care of it, Dan, and he did apologize. Something he's never done before. He even asked me to forgive him and help him change his ways."

"And that impressed you?" Dan seemed momentarily to have forgotten the reason he'd come.

"Impressing me had nothing to do with it. Like Brian said, a person doesn't always change their ways overnight, but at least he's willing to try."

"I see." Dan muttered the words, and Jenni chose to ignore the look of disgust on his face.

"Besides, we're not here about Brian, now are we?" she questioned, trying to get Dan to explain his appearance in the middle of the night.

"No, we're not," he agreed. He seemed to need a moment to think through his words, and so Jenni set to the task of pulling out her hairpins. Dan watched her in silence as she finished and ran her fingers through her long dark curls, as if to brush them into place.

Reaching over, Dan fingered a curl as he spoke, "I don't know where to begin."

"The beginning would be nice," Jenni tried to sound lighthearted.

"Do you remember the writers' conference I was asked to speak at?" Dan questioned.

"Of course," Jenni answered as she sat back against the couch.

"My publisher wanted very much for me to take the engagement. I didn't want to, but he scheduled me anyway and I finally agreed to do it." Dan's voice was troubled.

"When is it?" Jenni asked, unable to remember from their previous conversations.

"Next week," Dan said resolutely. "And I'm committed to speak at it."

"So what is the problem?"

"Do you remember I told you that they provided a list of questions I should be prepared to answer?" Jenni nodded and Dan continued. "I didn't feel that I could honestly answer some of those questions and I still don't. You've been after me a long time to talk honestly with you about many things. Believe me, there were times when all I wanted to do was forget my past agreements, my promises to others, and spill my guts."

Jenni's eyes narrowed slightly and a worried furrow lined her forehead. "What kind of promises?" she questioned suspiciously.

"Things I agree to do for my agent and publisher. Things I promised as a part of my contract," Dan answered honestly.

"Like what?"

"Well, for starters, I agreed to lie about my age." Jenni would have laughed if Dan hadn't been so serious. Before she could question him, though, Dan continued. "I was very young when I first started writing mysteries. My publisher and agent said that no one would find it believable that an eighteen-year-old could turn out such intense work. So, they told me to lie about my age."

"Dan, I hardly see the relevance in this. I mean I understand your commitment to your agent, although I know that lying is wrong, but I still don't see where I fit into this." Jenni felt a little exasperated.

"I lied about other things too, Jenni," Dan said, bowing his head. "I don't want to speak at that conference, because one of the questions on the list is, 'To what or whom do you credit your success?'"

"So?" Jenni questioned innocently.

"Jenni, I can't answer that question honestly because of my agreement," Dan began, "but if I don't answer it, I will betray a much greater commitment."

"Which is?" Jenni couldn't help but ask.

"My commitment to God, Jenni."

Jenni felt as if a tremendous weight had been lifted off not only her shoulders but his. Somehow, Dan's revelation was not all that surprising.

"Your commitment to God?" Jenni whispered. "You're a Christian, aren't you?" It was more a statement than a question.

"Yes. I accepted Christ when I was seven years old. I even gave serious thought to becoming a minister. That's how committed I was," Dan replied truthfully.

"Was?"

"I've lied for seven years, Jenni. Never mentioning God, never admitting to being His child. All because my publisher and agent felt it would harm my career. My books are intense mystery and espionage. They felt hearing that Dan James, the veteran writer of such thrillers, was a Christian, people would steer away and not buy my work. I agreed only because I thought at the time that my religious views were nobody else's business anyway. But now, after meeting you, and nearly losing you because I wouldn't admit my love of God, well, I just couldn't take it anymore." Dan paused for a moment. "And losing you is nothing compared to the alienation I've felt from my Father in heaven."

Jenni smiled broadly, not even realizing what she was doing. "What are you going to do?" she asked, the smile still on her face.

Dan looked at her for a moment, and he couldn't help but feel better. "You smile like you're enjoying this."

"I'm reveling in the answered prayer," she answered happily.

"I knew you'd be like this, all happy and smiles. I knew it would be right, but I don't know how I'll ever get through the writers' conference. I either have to denounce my faith or break my contract."

"Well, the Bible makes it clear that if you're ashamed of Christ, He'll be ashamed of you before his Father. Dan," Jenni said as she moved closer to him, "just trust God to work out the details. Haven't you hidden Him long enough? And in spite of everything, He's blessed you."

"That He has," Dan said, looking deep into Jenni's eyes. "More than I deserve."

"Then honor Him for it." Jenni's softly spoken words were a comfort. "And," Jenni added, "trust Him, Dan. You know He won't let you down."

fifteen

Dan left Jenni feeling as though a weight had been lifted from him. He knew that this last summer of deception was not the only thing that had bothered him; now that he was free at last of the lifetime of lies and evasions, he realized how heavily it had pressed on him. The cold night air penetrated his jacket, but not his heart. Picking up his pace, Dan moved quietly up the hill to his cabin.

The sound of a man's voice caught Dan's attention as he passed the backside of the pay phone. The voice belonged to Brian Givens, and when Jenni's name was mentioned, Dan paused to listen.

"You know it won't make any difference, Sonya," Brian was crooning. "I'll always love you, even if I have to marry Jennifer. It won't change a thing."

Dan began to seethe as he continued to listen. Brian was clearly playing games with Jennifer. Surprisingly, Dan wasn't as angry at Givens for lying to Jenni about his feelings as he was worried about why he had lied. Why was he stringing Jenni along like that?

Dan remained hidden behind the wooden phone booth. Feeling only a momentary guilt for eavesdropping, he was grateful for the position of the booth against tall wooden fencing.

"You know it's necessary. Look, Sonya, I told you I'd be back by the first, but I have to convince Jenni to marry me. Otherwise she'll never trust me enough," Brian explained.

"Trust him enough for what?" Dan couldn't help but wonder.

"Yeah, yeah, she bought it. She thinks I'm a dyed-in-the-wool, born-again lunatic, just like her and the rest of her crazy family." Brian paused, obviously listening to the person on the other end.

"It'll be a cinch," Brian said in a smug manner. "She's too stupid to figure out anything different. She's still the same pie-in-the-sky, rose-colored-glasses Jennifer. She'll believe whatever I tell her."

Dan wanted to jump the wall and render Brian Givens completely unconscious, but he knew that wasn't the answer. Given the fact that competition between him and Givens had already been intense, Dan doubted if he could make Jennifer understand his reasons for attacking Givens. Besides, he knew that God would provide another, better way to deal with Brian Givens.

"Are you kidding?" Brian was laughing softly. "You needn't worry about that, my love. She had a fit when I kissed her tonight. She's as much a prude as ever." He paused again and laughed at whatever was being said. "Well, I suppose I did get carried away, but I kept thinking of how badly I wanted you, Sonya." This apparently appeased the woman, and Dan could tell by Brian's comments that he was about to conclude his conversation.

"You just keep at the old man. Dog his every step and if it becomes a problem, get someone else to help you. But make sure it's someone you can trust. If Campbell finds out, he'll ruin both of us." Brian's tone was serious now, and Dan couldn't help but wonder what Brian and his accomplice planned for Jennifer's father.

Brian was telling the woman that he loved her, and Dan quickly raced up the hill to the seclusion of his cabin.

Entering the cabin, Dan switched on the light and went immediately to his notebook computer. He began to type down the entire exchange between Brian and his Sonya. If necessary, he'd rely on the transcript to tell Jennifer what had transpired.

Then a sickening feeling hit him. How could he tell her? It would have been difficult under normal circumstances, but with both men in obvious rivalry for Jenni's affections, Dan wasn't sure but what she'd think it was a ploy to discredit Brian.

Throughout the rest of the night, Dan tossed and turned in bed, ever aware that somewhere in the night, Brian Givens plotted to destroy Keith Campbell's career and Jenni's heart.

ã

The following morning Jenni rose early. After a quick shower, she braided her hair and dressed. Jeans and an oversized, blue fisherman's sweater were her choice for the day.

With a renewed zest, Jenni sat down to begin working with the day's computer entries. Just past eight o'clock, both Kelly and Pamela Walker put in an appearance.

"Aunt Pam!" Jenni exclaimed and got up to embrace the older woman.

"You look great," Pamela said as she returned Jenni's affectionate hug. "You too, Kelly."

Kelly smiled. "Thanks, boss."

"Jenni," Pam began, "I know you're planning to head home in a few days and I just wanted you to know that everything is set. I don't have a permanent manager, mostly because I keep hoping you'll stay on, but I did secure a temporary for the daytime. You're going to be available for the evening, right, Kelly?"

"That's right, Pam. I don't have a problem with it at all," Kelly assured both Pam and Jenni.

"Well, then," Pam continued, "if there's nothing else I can do for you, I'll take the print outs and receipts, and be on my way. Dave probably wonders what's taken me this long."

"It was good to see you, Aunt Pam. Will I see you again before I leave?" Jenni questioned.

"I doubt it, love. But tell your folks hello and congratulate your father for me. I'm already certain he'll win hands down."

"I will and thanks again," Jenni smiled. "I really have enjoyed this job. You may get me more permanent than you want me."

"That's not possible," Pamela Walker said as she headed out the door. "Just call if you need me. You have the number."

After a shared breakfast and brief devotion, Kelly bundled up and headed out to supervise the cleaning staff, while Jenni turned her attention back to the computer. She noted that this would be a heavy day for both departures and new arrivals. Those days were always exhausting for everyone.

Jenni entered the remaining information in the computer, and after manipulating the software to get the answers she sought, Jenni wrote down on a piece of paper that cabins three, nine, ten, nineteen, and twenty were still available.

Just then the phone rang, startling Jenni. "Hello, O'Reilly's," she said in her most business-like voice.

"Jenni?"

"Mom!" Jenni exclaimed in sheer joy. "What a surprise. How are you? How's Dad and the campaign?"

"Whoa, slow down. We're both great and the campaign looks good. The polls, for what they're worth, have Dad well in the lead. Landslide victory, is the word going around the State House."

"I'm glad," Jenni said in a relieved tone. Not being in Topeka, Jenni had very little information or feel for what the media and campaign opponents were doing to her father.

"Are you still coming on the first?" Anne Campbell

questioned her daughter.

"Yes, and I'll probably call before I leave here." Jenni confirmed.

"Your father isn't very excited about you driving all that way alone."

"I won't be alone—remember God is my Co-pilot," Jenni replied, trying to soothe her mother's worried mind. "And who knows, maybe Brian will ride back with me." Jenni hesitated, remembering the previous night's events. "Then again," she said, deciding she'd rather not be alone with Brian for the long ride to Topeka, "I doubt that very seriously."

"Brian? Brian Givens?" Ann said in disbelief. "What is he doing there?"

"I figured he told you. After all, didn't you tell him where I was?" Jenni asked, rather surprised.

"Not at all. I figured he was still working on the Jenson and Lee campaigns. I certainly didn't know he'd come out there to bother you. Are you okay?" Jenni's mother was clearly worried about Brian's arrival in Estes Park.

"I'm doing fine, Mom. Really I am. Did you know that Brian has become a Christian?" Jenni questioned curiously.

"No, I hadn't heard anything about that," her mother replied. "When did this happen?"

"He told me it happened sometime this fall. He said he realized that the things I'd told him about God were true and that he knew he was lost." Jenni paused, hesitating to say that Brian had renewed his interest in their relationship. Should she further worry her mother with that bit of news?

"So why did he come all the way out there to tell you that?" Ann Campbell asked suspiciously. "Wouldn't a phone call have sufficed?"

"I suppose," Jenni said with deliberate slowness, "it had more to do with the fact that he wanted to win me back, as he put it."

"Oh, Jenni, you aren't considering it, are you? Even if he has accepted Christ, I—" Her mother fell silent, as though hesitant to finish her thought.

"I don't think I could ever resume our relationship, Mom. Not after the way I was hurt. But I've gone out with him a few times." That was an understatement, Jenni thought to herself. Morning, noon and night, Brian was plaguing her for one reason or another. "But, I don't feel the same way I used to."

"Please promise me you'll be careful, Jenni. I really don't trust him. I mean, I hope his confession is true and I pray that he has found a way to turn his life around, but, Jenni, please be careful. Remember that you'll know them by their fruit."

"I will, Mom. I better go now. I love you."

She was just putting the receiver back in place when Brian came bounding into the office with a bright smile on his face.

"Good morning, beautiful. Sleep well?" he questioned with a glint in his eye.

"It was a rather short night," Jenni said, returning his smile. "But yes, I did sleep well. In fact I feel as though I could walk over Trail Ridge Road and back. If it weren't already snow packed, I'd probably try it too."

"Why all this enthusiasm?" Brian questioned, leaning down with his elbows on the office counter.

"Oh, I don't know," Jenni said avoiding his eyes. How could she tell him that Dan's confession had given her heart wings to soar on? "I guess it's because I just heard from my mother." It wasn't the whole truth, but it certainly wasn't a lie.

"Oh?" Brian seemed intently interested. "How are things going back home?"

"Great, just great. Mom says they expect Daddy to win by a landslide. I never doubted it for a minute though." Jenni's pride in her father was evident.

Brian hid a frown and pretended to cough. "Well, then, since you're already in good spirits, how about my capping off the morning with something even better?"

"It's only nine-thirty, no need to cap anything off yet," Jenni teased. "Besides what could be better than hearing good news from home?"

"How about this?" Brian said, opening a small jewelry box to reveal a diamond ring.

"Oh," Jenni said.

"Oh? Is that all you have to say?" he teased.

"I don't know what to say, Brian."

"Say yes," Brian prodded. "Just say yes."

But Jenni was already miles away. She couldn't help but think of the last time she'd said yes to Brian's proposal of marriage. Nor could she put the blue-eyed Daniel James from her mind.

"Wha—what?" she stammered, realizing that Brian was speaking to her.

Brian placed the ring box on the counter and came around to pull Jenni into his arms. "I said, marry me. Today, tonight, tomorrow! I don't care, just say you will."

He lowered his lips to kiss Jenni tenderly, with none of the urgent passion that had nearly destroyed her opinion of him the night before. Jenni's mind reeled as she tried to sort through the feelings and emotions of the moment. *Marry Brian?*

"I guess I'm the one who picked the wrong time to interrupt this time," Dan said as he stood not two feet behind Brian.

Jenni pushed away from Brian and met Dan's pain-filled eyes. She'd not heard the bells on the front door, nor Dan's footsteps as he'd entered. Brian seemed to be enjoying the moment very much and said nothing.

"I—I—" Jenni stammered to find words to take the sting out of what Dan had observed.

"No need to explain," Dan said with a fleeting smile. "I just came to invite you to the writers' conference. It'll keep." Dan moved toward the door.

"No, wait!" Jenni cried out, realizing she sounded desperate. "Don't leave yet."

"Yes, James," Brian added with a superior satisfaction to his voice. "Help us celebrate."

"Celebrate?" Dan questioned Brian's words but his eyes never left Jennifer.

"Yes, celebrate. I've just asked Jenni to become my wife!"

sixteen

Jenni hated the look on Dan's face. His eyes looked first to her and then to Brian, and in their depths was an expression of betrayal.

"He asked," Jenni said quickly, "but I haven't answered." Her eyes pleaded with Dan to understand. She turned then to Brian and reprimanded him, "You assume too much, Brian. I'm not ready to agree to marry you."

"Well, this ring certainly ought to help you make up your mind." Brian flashed the ring under Dan's nose.

"The ring is lovely, Brian, but that will have little to do with my decision. Now, if both of you will excuse me, I have work to do," Jenni said and took a seat behind the desk counter.

Leaning over the counter, Dan whispered, "Whatever you decide, give yourself plenty of time to make the right choice."

Jenni smiled. The look on Dan's face betrayed his feelings for her. "I will," she promised. With a nod of his head toward Brian, Dan left the cabin.

"What was all that about?" Brian questioned.

"I told you I have work to do, Brian. Now I want you to go." Jenni pointed to the door.

"But I just asked you to marry me!"

"I know," Jenni replied.

"And?" Brian was trying his best to control his temper.

"And what?" Jenni questioned as she looked up from the computer. "I can't give you an answer just like that." Jenni snapped her fingers.

"But, Jenni," Brian began, "this shouldn't be all that hard.

We were engaged for two years. We've only been apart for a few months. How hard of a decision could it be? Either you love me or you don't."

"Brian, I need time to think."

"Think about what?" Brian ranted with his arms raised. "What's the problem here, Jenni? It's him, isn't it?" The look on Jenni's face left Brian little doubt that he was right.

"Dan has become very important to me," Jenni remarked. "Now, if you don't mind—"

"Do you love him?" Brian interrupted.

"What?" Jenni was taken aback by the question. "I don't believe that's any of your business. My feelings and thoughts are personal in this matter." Then, getting up from the desk, she turned to leave. "If I can't work here, I'll go where I can."

Jenni went to the laundry room and started folding towels and sheets. Brian's sudden announcement had shocked her, while Dan's pain-filled expression had broken her heart. She finished with the laundry, and after giving the room a good cleaning, she made her way outside. Without giving it a second thought, she found herself headed up the hill toward Dan's cabin.

A light dusting of snow had covered the porch, but Jenni knew it would be gone as soon as the sun was high enough in the sky. Even in summer, they sometimes got snow in the wee hours of the morning.

Jenni knocked lightly on the door and waited. For a moment she wondered if Dan had gone hiking. He was pretty upset and she couldn't really blame him. Brian had sounded as if he and she were well on their way to the church.

Dan opened the door and smiled. "I hoped you'd come up. I even prayed about it."

"Kind of a selfish prayer, wasn't it?" Jenni grinned,

entering the cabin.

"I was just thinking about the 'desires of my heart' and things along those lines. Can I get you something? Coffee? Diet pop? Me?" He gave her a wink of his eye, and his tone left Jenni breathless. He went to the refrigerator to look for something else to offer, while Jenni studied him, unable to turn away.

Dan suddenly realized that Jenni was observing him, and with a cocky tilt of his head, he teased, "Lose something?"

Jenni blushed as she realized how blatant her study had been, and tried desperately to change the subject. "I want—want you. . ." she stammered.

"You what?" Dan grinned, thoroughly enjoying her discomfort. "I mean, I came up here to let you know, I. . ." Jenni fell silent. Her eyes locked with Dan's incredibly blue ones, and all she could think about was how much she really did love this man. How could she even consider marrying Brian? And yet somehow she felt she was obligated to consider his proposal. Or was she? Did she owe Brian anything?

Dan crossed the distance between them but stopped short of taking Jenni into his arms. He was making this most difficult, Jenni decided. Throwing pride to the wind, she threw her arms around his neck and pulled his head down to hers.

Jenni was also the one to instigate the kiss, a sweet kiss of deep, heart-felt longing. Without giving much thought to the consequences, Jenni blurted, "I think I'm in love with you."

She half-expected Dan to tell her the same, and when he didn't, she dropped her arms and turned to leave.

"Whoa! Where do you think you're going?" Dan asked, pulling her back into his arms.

"I can't think clearly," Jenni answered. She was hurt by his lack of response to her declaration.

"You can't just waltz into a man's house, throw yourself at

him, tell him you think you love him—and then walk out. You have a little bit of explaining to do, Miss Campbell." The glint in his eyes told Jenni that he was teasing, but her heart still held an awful dread that her calculations of Dan's feelings for her might be wrong.

"I shouldn't have said that," Jenni whispered, while Dan led her to a small couch.

"Why? Didn't you mean it?" Dan's voice was serious.

"It's not that," Jenni said with her head bowed. She could feel tears forming in her eyes. She truly didn't want to break down in front of this man.

"Look at me," Dan commanded.

Jenni shook her head, so afraid that if she saw rejection in his eyes or heard him say something to cast off her feelings, she'd burst into tears on the spot.

Dan gently cupped Jenni's chin and lifted her face. She closed her eyes tightly, trying to blink back the tears. "Look at me," he whispered gently.

She opened her eyes, revealing the tears that now dripped from her black lashes. Dan's face held a puzzled look for a moment.

"I have to go," Jenni said in a barely audible voice.

"No, you don't, you're the boss here. Remember?" Dan replied as he brushed away a single teardrop that slid down her cheek. "Now, what's all this about?"

Jenni shrugged and tried to slide away from Dan's close presence. "It's just been a hard day—and look, it's only ten-thirty," she tried to joke. The tone of her voice showed that she was on the verge of losing her ability to remain collected.

"Can't you tell me why you're so upset?" Dan questioned as he allowed her to put distance between them. "Is it Brian?"

"No, not really. Oh, I wasn't expecting *his* actions either," Jenni said without thinking.

"Either? What's that supposed to mean?"

Jenni felt herself growing warm under Dan's scrutiny. How could she explain that she had hoped to hear some word of love pass from his lips? How could she tell him how much it had cost her just to say the words she had spoken?

"I—it's just that—oh, never mind," Jenni said and got up quickly to leave.

Dan vaulted over the back of the couch and blocked her way to the door. "Are you going to tell me what all this is about? I think I deserve some kind of explanation after this morning."

"This morning?" Jenni questioned, jerking her head up. "This morning?" she repeated.

"That's right. Your little engagement party with Mr. Givens. Do you have any idea how awkward that was?" Dan questioned. "And now you're acting mighty strange if you ask me." He wanted so much to tell Jenni about overhearing Brian's phone conversation and how he knew that Brian was just using her. But instead, he tried to keep the subject focused just on her.

"Well, nobody's asking," Jenni said defensively. She crossed her arms across her chest as Dan took a step forward.

"I didn't mean it like that. I just want to know that you're okay. I care, you know." Dan was thinking how hurt Jenni would be when she learned that Brian was planning on keeping a mistress, even if he married Jenni.

"You care?" Jenni said feigning shock. "Who could tell?"

"Sarcasm? From you? That doesn't seem quite right."

Dan's words so irritated Jenni that her fear passed into anger. "Nothing seems quite right. I come in here and spill out my heart to you, and you—you—" Jenni's temper was obvious and Dan's eyes opened wide as he realized that her anger was directed at his lack of response to her earlier declaration.

"You mean all this is about me and what I said?" Dan was starting to enjoy himself again, now that he was no longer worried about Jenni's feeling in regard to Brian Givens.

"Not at all, Mr. James. It wasn't what you said, it was what you didn't say," Jenni said, pushing past him and reaching for the door.

Dan gave out a hearty laugh, and opened the door for her. "I tell you what, Jennifer Campbell. You come back when you no longer just 'think' you love me, and we'll discuss it."

"Oh, you're insufferable," Jenni said, hazel eyes blazing fire. "You really are." She pushed past him, even as he continued to laugh.

She was halfway back to the office when it suddenly dawned on her that he hadn't objected to her affections, he only wanted her to be sure of them. Maybe he was wiser than she gave him credit for.

seventeen

The next day was Jenni's turn to sleep late, but before she could awaken on her own, Kelly was lightly knocking at her door.

"Come in," Jenni said, yawning as Kelly entered her bedroom. "Sorry, I just can't seem to wake up."

"Well, maybe this will do it?" Kelly said. Jenni realized Kelly was holding a long-stemmed red rose and a card.

"Brian?" Jenni grimaced.

"No, Dan."

"Really? Dan sent it?" Jenni suddenly found herself wide awake.

Kelly laughed out loud. "Yes. Dan was here just a few moments ago and he asked me to see that you got this right away. He said it was important and pertained to something happening today."

Jenni opened the card and found a pass to the writers' conference, along with Dan's hastily scrawled invitation. "He wants me to come hear his speech at two o'clock." Jenni murmured, reading the note. "He says it's important to him, especially since I was the one who helped him come to terms with not hiding his faith in God."

"I think you should definitely go," Kelly said enthusiastically. "You may be sorry if you don't. Besides," she added, "he probably needs the moral support."

"You're probably right," Jenni agreed. She hadn't thought of that. Given the fact that his publisher and agent had adamantly refused to allow him this privilege for so many years,

143

he was bound to be feeling some trepidation at the prospect of admitting his faith at last.

"Then you're going?" Kelly asked curiously.

"I believe I will," Jenni decided. "I suppose I should go up and tell him."

Kelly shook her head. "He's not there. He told me he'd be tied up in workshops this morning. That's why it was important that he stop by first thing this morning."

"Oh," Jenni said, trying to hide her disappointment.

"Look," Kelly said, "you just go and have a good time and I'll be fine here. We don't have a big load at all and even the cleaning will be a cinch because most of the guests are weekers. We won't have any thorough cleaning to do until next weekend."

"I'd nearly forgotten about the resort," Jenni had to admit. "On top of everything else, with me going home for several days, I wanted to give you as much time off as possible before I left."

"Not a problem," Kelly tried to convince Jenni. "Besides, I'd rather have some extra time at Thanksgiving."

"Well, you can certainly have that," Jenni confirmed. "I'll see to it if I have to clean all twenty-one cabins and run this office by myself."

"In that case, you'd better get around and decide what you're going to wear. It'll be two before you know it."

❧

At exactly five before two, Jenni walked into the conference center's main auditorium. She presented her pass at the door and was ushered to the front of the room. When she tried to protest and suggest that she sit toward the back, the usher assured her that this type of pass gave her a special seating arrangement.

Jenni shrugged her shoulders and allowed the man to seat

her close to the front and center of the auditorium. She had hoped to see Dan before his speech, but time had gotten away from her at O'Reilly's, and suddenly she had found herself hard pressed just to get here on time.

Jenni glanced around nervously. She didn't know anyone here; she could only surmise that most were budding young authors looking for bits of advice and trade secrets.

"If you'll take your seats," an older, white-haired man was announcing, "we'll get started." He looked quite distinguished in his brown tweed suit jacket with suede patches at the elbows. Just like all writers should look, Jenni mused to herself.

"As you all know," the man continued, "we've been very fortunate to get Daniel James to address the convention this year." At this a thunderous applause filled the auditorium and stunned Jenni. These people apparently loved Dan's writing as much as she did.

"I'm sure that many of you attended his workshop on the successful plotting of a mystery." Again applause. Jenni couldn't help but smile.

"Without further ado, I'd like to welcome Daniel James to our fifteenth annual writers' conference." The applause was louder than ever as an immaculately dressed Dan appeared stage left and walked to the podium.

Jenni felt her breath catch as he winked at her before he turned to greet the convention crowd. He was stunning in his dark blue business suit, white shirt, and red and blue striped tie. He looked every bit the part of the successful writer. Jenni thought he made a striking figure, but to herself she admitted that she preferred him in his more casual jeans and sweaters.

"Thank you very much for the warm response," Dan was saying as he began his address. "You have made me feel very welcome today and I especially want to thank Dr. Richards for putting this conference together and inviting me." The white-haired man who'd introduced Daniel and now sat at the end of the platform, stood and gave a slight bow of acknowledgement to the applauding crowd.

Dan smiled warmly at Jenni, leaving her weak. He seemed so determined, so different somehow, that Jenni found herself trying to figure out why his eyes held a glint of something mysterious in them.

"When I was first asked to speak here, I wasn't inclined to accept. Now, before you prejudge my reasons, I want to share with you exactly why I felt that way. Many of you don't realize this, but I'm only twenty-five. I've been published and lauded as a meritable mystery writer since the age of eighteen. Now I share this with you for two reasons. One, I'm laying the foundation for the real meat of my speech here today, and secondly, I want to encourage everyone here that age is no factor when you have something to say."

Jenni noticed there was some good-natured comments made amongst the older people in the crowd, as well as genuine looks of encouragement on the faces of the younger writer-hopefuls.

"Most of you have believed me to be anywhere from twenty-eight to thirty-eight. This was a ploy by my agent to make me more appealing to a broader range of readers. At the time, it seemed like a good idea to me. After all, who would want to read the works of a child?"

Dan paused for a moment and then continued, "When you asked me to speak, I was given a list of questions I should address during my speech. This very list nearly turned me away from accepting." There was a murmuring amongst the auditorium crowd, and Jenni knew how difficult this moment was for Dan.

"The reason," Dan said with a firm and clear voice, "was

that one question I could not come and speak honestly about. This question had to do with what I attribute my success to."

Jenni felt herself nearly holding her breath as Dan continued. "You see, I attribute my success to Someone very dear and special to me. Someone who has seen me through the worst times, as well as the best ones. However, my publisher had convinced me for over seven years to remain silent about this. The reason has been concern that I would lose my reader market, and public interest would wane if people realized that I accredited Jesus Christ with my success."

Jenni noticed that dead silence fell across the room. "You see," Dan continued, "when I was a young man of seven, I accepted Jesus Christ as my personal Savior—and just like Robert Frost's two roads, it has made all the difference."

Dan stepped from behind the podium, taking the microphone with him, and walked down the stage steps until he was level with the auditorium crowd. "I'm not talking about getting religious or churchy or anything that sounds as undesirable as all that. I'm speaking of a day by day walk with the best Friend a person could ever have. I'm talking about a young boy who needed that Friend desperately because his father had walked out and left his mother with four young children to care for. A boy who needed to believe that not all fathers were bad and that not all those who loved you would leave you."

Jenni felt her eyes well up with tears as she listened to Dan's story. "My mother was unskilled and unable to provide for her children. When my father left, we were plunged further into poverty, as well as a filthy, crime-filled neighborhood. Drugs were important to nearly every neighbor and prostitution ran rampant. I know that without Jesus, I would have been bitter and angry. Two days before my mother died, my only brother took his life because he couldn't deal with the anger he felt towards God."

At this Jenni heard several gasps, including her own. How awful to lose so many people that you loved.

"I was seventeen at the time and my brother was fifteen. He hadn't found peace as I had and he refused to listen to me when I tried so desperately to share the Gospel with him. Now, lest you think that this is a sermon, it's not. I simply needed to explain to you that my walk with Christ is much more than a religious experience. Jesus Christ is my life."

Jenni wanted to cheer and clap, but somehow found a way to restrain herself. Dan was standing less than ten feet away and she wished very much that she could let him know how much she cared.

"I can't address you people today without sharing with you that without Jesus I'd be nothing. Oh, I might still write the occasional book, I might even be as popular a writer as I am at this point in my career—but none of it would matter because no matter how much money I made or how many books I sold, the emptiness would smother me if I had to live without my heavenly Father's love."

Jenni found herself clapping and suddenly the entire room joined her. The applause was loud and long, and Dan fairly beamed from the acknowledgement that the crowd approved his right to be a Christian and to speak out for the God he loved.

After several more comments, Jenni found herself suddenly looking face to face with Dan. "I have to share with you," he was saying as he walked closer to Jenni, "a very important person in my life. A person I believe God has sent my way to spend the rest of my life with." He was now reaching out for Jenni, but her trembling hand could barely reach up to his.

"This is Jennifer Campbell," Dan said as he pulled Jenni to his side, "the woman I hope will one day be my wife."

Jenni's head snapped up in surprise. "What?" she whispered against the thunderous applause of the auditorium.

Dan's mischievous grin was very close as he leaned toward her. "Well?" he murmured against her ear.

Jenni felt her knees begin to wobble. Her chest felt tight and her mind raced a million miles a minute. Dan James had just proposed in front of over two hundred people.

With tears blurring her eyes, Jenni knew she had to get out of the room. Dan had returned to the front of the room to finish his speech and take questions. As soon as people began to raise their hands, Jenni slipped out the side aisle and ran for the seclusion of her car.

eighteen

Jenni drove back to O'Reilly's in a stupor. Wasn't this what she'd wanted? Hadn't she been dreaming that Dan would one day propose to her? Yet here it had happened, and she only felt frustration and confusion.

As she pulled into her customary parking place, she turned off the engine and began to pray. "I need You so much, Father. I need You to show me what the right decision is. Now that Daniel has proposed, I'm more perplexed than ever. Just when I think my feelings are clear, Brian's image fills my head. What should I do, Lord?"

Suddenly, Jenni thought of several verse from I John 3:10. She found herself whispering them aloud to remind herself of their wisdom in her situation. "This is how we know who the children of God are and who the children of the devil are: Anyone who does not do what is right is not a child of God; neither is anyone who does not love his brother."

Jenni thought for several moments before continuing her prayer. "But, Father, both men claim to be Your children. Both claim to have given their lives over to You by accepting Jesus as their Savior." Her eyes filled with tears from the frustration of the moment. "I don't know what to do!"

A tap on the window so startled Jenni that she jumped. When she turned her head, she was relieved to find Kelly at the door. Jenni opened the car door and stepped into Kelly's open arms. As she sobbed, Kelly offered her consolation.

"You aren't going to believe this, but Dan asked me to marry him," Jenni sobbed.

"That's good, isn't it?" Kelly questioned with a smile.

"Oh, Kelly, I want it to be. I thought it was all I wanted, but since Brian asked me too, I just don't know what to think."

"Do you love Brian?" Kelly asked.

"I don't know. I can't really figure out what it is I feel for Brian. I feel happy that he's found the Lord. It pleases me that he's a part of God's family. I also have some good memories with Brian that make me feel good. I don't think I completely trust him, though. I care *about* him, but I'm not sure I care *for* him. There is a difference, isn't there?" Jenni questioned.

"I think so," Kelly confirmed. "What about Dan? Do you love him?"

"Yes, I'm fairly certain that I love him," Jenni said, shaking her head.

"Fairly certain? What's that supposed to mean?"

"Well, I think I love him in the right way. You know, in more than just a physical way. It's just that the physical attraction between us tends to cloud my thinking." Jenni frowned and then continued, "Anyway, I think the love I feel for him is genuine. I don't feel it out of obligation and I don't feel intimidated by him. I'm just not sure. I feel so confused by my physical reaction to him."

"But you do feel intimidated by Brian?" Kelly questioned.

Jenni had never really thought those words before, but she had to acknowledge now that they were true. "Yes, I suppose I do."

"Look," Kelly said as she took hold of Jenni's hand, "I'm going to pray with you and then I think the best thing for everyone is for you to go on home. Go back to Topeka today. Why wait until tomorrow? I can manage just fine here and this way you can leave without having to see or talk to either Daniel or Brian."

"Do you think it would help?" Jenni questioned.

"I think it would give you over six hundred miles to pray in solitude," Kelly said and squeezed Jenni's hand. "And you know that can't hurt."

≈

Interstate 70 stretched out before her, a long gray ribbon leading to the horizon. Once Denver was well behind her, the land became flat and desolate. She passed an occasional small town, but nothing of any major proportion until Limon, Colorado, where Jenni spent the night.

The next morning, Jenni rose early and after a light breakfast hurried to get back to the highway. She drove ever closer to Topeka, while a light snow fell.

When she was only two hours from home, she decided to stop in Abilene for dinner. Spotting a steak house, she pulled into the parking lot and went inside. She freshened up in the rest room, then allowed the hostess to seat her in the dining room. Jenni couldn't suppress a yawn as the waitress placed a glass of water on the table and offered her a menu.

"Where ya'll bound tonight?" the woman questioned.

"Topeka," Jenni answered, looking the menu over.

"Well, you're almost there," the waitress offered. "What can I get you?"

The woman took her order, then left for a moment and quickly returned with a pot of steaming coffee. Pouring Jenni a cup, she asked, "Would you like a newspaper to read while you wait for dinner?"

Jenni shook her head. "I'm not too familiar with Abilene."

"We've got the Topeka paper too."

Jenni perked up. "In that case, I'd love to." The older woman smiled and quickly retrieved a copy for Jenni.

Jenni smiled at the familiar newspaper as the waitress said, "It'll be about fifteen minutes before your steak is ready. You want me to wait your salad until it's ready or do you want it now?"

"I'd rather just wait, thanks," Jenni said and started to read through the headlines of her hometown paper.

She had covered the first few pages, when a photograph caught her attention. Some of the faces were familiar. Looking closer, Jenni recognized several of the people in the photograph.

Two of the women were friends she'd made through college. While they hadn't been all that close, they were nonetheless friends. The other face she recognized was Brian's. He stood with his arm casually draped across the shoulder of a striking, dark-haired woman. The woman was exotic-looking with her dark eyes, and she was smiling up at Brian with a look that made Jenni certain they were more than just acquaintances.

She felt a lump in her throat as she read the caption: GIVENS TO JOIN WASHINGTON LOBBY GROUP. Why hadn't Brian mentioned this before? Jenni willed herself to read the article which explained Brian's plans to join the Washington, DC, group by the first of the new year. At that time he intended to fight for hazardous waste restrictions.

Jenni read on. The woman in the picture with Brian was Sonya Elbertson, the daughter of a well-known socialite in Washington. The paper implied that Sonya and Brian were quite an item. Glancing at the top of the page, Jenni noted that the paper held yesterday's date. What did it mean? Brian had been in Estes for the last few weeks.

When the food arrived, Jenni ate quickly. She left the waitress a generous tip, paid for her meal, and with the newspaper picture planted firmly in her mind, she headed for Topeka.

Darkness had fallen and her watch read eight-thirty when

Jenni finally pulled into the familiar driveway of her parents' Victorian home. For a moment after turning off the engine, Jenni just sat back and took it all in.

The lights were on in the front room as well as in Julie's room upstairs. She tried to imagine that her parents were sitting in the living room enjoying a quiet evening, but Jenni knew the truth.

Most likely her parents weren't even home yet. They were probably at one public appearance or another. Things were always hectic in the last few days before an election, and now with the election just days away, Jenni knew her father would be a hard man to catch up with.

Finally, Jenni found the energy to get out of the car and climb the steps of her parents' house. Funny, how it no longer seemed to be her house too.

ea

Jenni had been right about her parents' absence. Not until the night before the election did Jenni finally get a chance to talk to her mother and father alone.

"It's good to have you here," Keith Campbell told his older daughter. He good-naturedly teased her about moving off to the mountains and then questioned her about her plans.

"I'm not sure what I'm going to do," she began honestly. "That was one of the reasons I came home early. I have a real dilemma and I need your help."

"What's the problem, honey?" Jenni's mom put a protective arm around her daughter's shoulder.

"Well, it would seem that two different, very different, men have asked me to marry them." Jenni waited until the shocked expressions on her parents' faces faded into curiosity.

"Go on," Keith motioned his daughter. "Who are these men?"

"One is Brian Givens. The other is the writer I told you

about, Dan James." Jenni offered the information, knowing that her parents wouldn't be pleased to hear Brian's name on the roll.

"Brian asked you to marry him again?" Anne Campbell asked warily.

"Yes. He told me that he'd become a Christian and that it was all because of what I'd told him, and how I'd lived, that caused him to give his life to Christ," Jenni explained.

"Brian?" Keith questioned, looking first at Jenni and then to his wife. "A Christian? Are you sure he actually said he'd become a Christian, not that he just *understood* your beliefs as a Christian?"

"No," Jenni confirmed. "He told me that he'd accepted Jesus as his Savior."

Keith Campbell looked troubled. "I don't want to judge him falsely, Jennifer, but his actions don't exactly bespeak that of a Christian man."

"Well, I know what you mean," Jennifer began. "He was rather obnoxious with me a couple of times, but he reminded me that it's hard to change overnight. I guess I wanted to give him the benefit of the doubt."

"That's admirable, but perhaps not very realistic in this case," Keith said with a seriousness to his voice that alarmed Jenni.

"What is it, Daddy? What do you know?"

"Only rumors at this point, although there is an investigation going on. It is in the utmost of confidence that I share any of this with you. It's believed that Brian paid for his law credentials, and furthermore, that this environmental company he's going to work for is actually responsible for illegal toxic waste dumping." Keith spoke in a hushed tone. Although they were in the privacy of the family den, he knew that to divulge such secret information was seldom wise.

"So you don't believe that Brian has accepted Christ?"

"No, I don't," Keith admitted. "God forgive me if I'm bearing him undue prejudice, but Givens has a great deal to gain by having you for his wife."

"Such as?" Jenni questioned.

"Such as I'm the one heading the investigation into his actions. If you were to marry him, Brian would naturally assume that you would get me to call off the investigation—or at least find in his favor."

Jenni looked stunned. "Is he in all that much trouble? So much that he'd come to Colorado to seek me out and lie to me?"

"He stands to lose everything he's worked for," Keith answered simply. "Desperation in men breeds desperate actions. I believe Brian Givens would stop at nothing to see his dream accomplished."

Suddenly, Jennifer remembered the woman in the picture. "Who is Sonya Elbertson?"

Anne Campbell exchanged a worried look with her husband. "She has been Brian's constant companion. After he broke the engagement with you and you went to Colorado, it was only a matter of a day or two before Sonya appeared on his arm."

"I see," Jenni said softly. Unfortunately, she was beginning to see more than she wanted—and the picture wasn't very nice.

nineteen

Keith Campbell had always chosen to hold a small party at his house on election night, and this year was no exception. Jenni readied herself for the evening's events, feeling confident her father would again secure his seat in the House.

The party would be rather informal, though Jenni knew everyone would look their best. She chose an ecru wool sweater with drop-shoulders and dainty seedstitching. To go with this Jenni had picked out a multi-gored, rayon skirt of the same color.

She carefully pinned her hair up and pulled a few wisps around her face to take away any hint of severity. Looking in the mirror, Jenni was pleased with her appearance and knew that her parents would be too. She slipped on a pair of matching hose and heels before descending to the party downstairs.

Jenni was amazed at the number of people already milling about her home. She had purposefully joined the party late, in order to avoid Brian for as long as possible. She knew that he had wrangled an invitation from her father, probably hoping to get in his good graces.

But even though she already knew he'd be there, she still wasn't prepared for actually meeting with him. "Jennifer," he called from somewhere behind her, and Jenni wished most desperately that she could just continue walking away.

Instead she turned to greet him. "Hello, Brian," she said, trying not to sound as cold as she felt.

Brian approached her with an appraising smile. "You look

exquisite. I'm a very lucky man to have you by my side to-night."

Jenni frowned. "I'm not here to be at your side tonight. I'm here for my father."

"Of course," Brian cooed, "but you are going to announce our engagement, aren't you?"

Jenni jerked away. "Certainly not. I don't plan to make announcements of any sort. This is Daddy's night and I won't stand in his limelight." She moved to walk away, but found Brian quickly in tow.

"Look," he began. "I didn't mean to upset you. I just assumed that since you left Estes in such a hurry, that it meant you'd made up your mind."

Jenni whirled around to face him. "I have, but my decision wasn't to marry you. In fact, I don't even know why you're here. You don't like my father's politics."

Brian glanced around the room. Several people were staring at the couple. Hoping to avoid further stares, Brian pulled Jenni down the hallway to one of the off-limit sections of the house.

"Brian, let go of me," Jenni insisted when Brian finally stopped.

"Not until you listen to me. You aren't making any sense. I have to help you see that things will only get harder for your family if you don't marry me."

"Are you threatening my family's welfare?" Jenni asked indignantly.

"Not me, Jen. But I can protect them from things and people. You just don't understand how it works in politics." Brian's voice was soft. He had backed her up against the hallway wall, until Jenni felt her head make contact with one of the portraits hanging there.

"I've lived in politics all my life, Brian. It's you who's standing on the outside looking in. I know all about dirty schemes and mud slinging. I'm not the simpleton you wish I were."

"I know you're a smart cookie," Brian said, planting his hands firmly on the wall on each side of her head.

"Back off, Brian," she said, trying to sound firm. "You don't want this kind of scene here, tonight." The look in Brian's eyes made it clear that she'd struck a nerve. "It wouldn't help your career at all to be thrown out of our house, but so help me that's what'll happen."

Brian shrugged his shoulders and pulled away. "I'm only trying to remind you of what we have going together."

"We have nothing, Brian. We have nothing now and we had nothing in the past."

"But we could, if you'd only let us. I want to be the kind of man that you need. I want to do the right things, but—Jenni, I need you, and I love you," he whispered.

"I don't want to talk about this now," Jenni said and walked quickly back to the party.

The rest of the evening was spoiled for her. All Jenni could think about were the things her parents had told her about Brian—and then in contrast, Brian's flowery declaration of love.

Jenni found herself smiling for the party but crying out to God on the inside, *Where is the truth, Lord?*

As the evening progressed, Jenni worked harder and harder to avoid Brian. She was trying desperately to get caught up in the happy mood of her parents, when she noted a late arriving guest standing in the front doorway. It was Sonya Elbertson.

Jenni was shocked to see her, but that shock was nothing compared to the display Sonya made when she took off her full-length mink coat. Beneath the coat Sonya wore a daringly risqué black mini-dress that bore a striking resemblance to a slip. Her make-up was heavy and her jewelry glittered, giving her the type of appearance that demanded attention.

Jenni moved back into the crowd of people as Sonya was ushered into the house and greeted by Keith and Anne Campbell. Funny that her parents had said nothing about inviting Sonya to the party. Jenni found herself keeping a wary eye on Sonya and Brian throughout the evening, watching and waiting for something to happen.

At ten o'clock, Keith was declared a winner by the news media, and the television cameras were already in place to interview him. Usually Jenni joined her parents and sister on the podium, but not tonight. She ducked out down the off-limits hallway and through a back entrance to the alcove just off the kitchen.

Coming through the darkened doorway, Jenni was surprised to hear voices. No one was supposed to be in this part of the house, and Jenni was nearly ready to snap on the lights when she recognized Brian's voice.

"Oh, Sonya," he murmured, his voice thick with passion. "I've missed you so much."

"How much longer will you have to play at this charade?" Sonya questioned in a sultry, breathless voice. "Um, I love it when you do that."

Jenni felt her cheeks burn in embarrassment. She wanted to back out the doorway before they discovered her presence, but something seemed to hold her fast to the spot.

"Why don't we blow this thing and go to your motel room?" Brian whispered.

"What about your little prudish wife-to-be?" Sonya fairly purred. "Won't she be bothered by your absence?"

"Well, to tell you the truth, Jennifer Campbell may prove to be difficult. I'm beginning to wonder if I'm going about this the wrong way."

"Nonsense. You know what Father told you. Marry her and use it to our advantage. We'll only need it to be that way for a year, maybe two."

Jenni felt tears flow down her cheeks. She wasn't mourning the loss of love between herself and Brian, she realized, but the loss of innocence. She'd been so sheltered all her life, even in the midst of the political scene that held her family captive. Until now, she had never known that people could be as completely devoid of morals or values as she now saw that Brian Givens was.

"But, Sonya," Brian began, "I don't know if I can go through with it. I don't play this Christian thing very well, and I haven't the foggiest idea of how to keep it up after we're married. Oh, I know nothing will change between you and me but—"

"Of course it won't change," Sonya interrupted. "I'll always love you and you know very well I don't mind playing second fiddle while you secure our future."

"You'll never play second fiddle to anyone," Brian said passionately. Jenni could tell that Brian and Sonya were kissing. "I'll get this thing resolved," Brian said after a moment. "I'll marry Keith Campbell's daughter, then I'll fix him once and for all."

"Good," Sonya whispered. "Now about that motel room. . ."

Jenni ducked out of the alcove and ran for the haven of her bedroom. She didn't even bother to turn on the lights as she entered the room and slammed the door behind her. She was as angry and hurt as she'd been when Brian had ended their engagement.

"No," she said aloud, "I'm even madder than that."

She paced back and forth in her room for a moment, letting her tears flow freely. How could she have been so foolish? She wished desperately that she could talk to someone, but everyone was busy with the election. The one person she wanted to talk to, to hold right that minute, was over six hundred miles away.

"I'll call him," she announced to the darkened room. She turned on the small desk lamp and dialed the number for O'Reilly's. Just hearing the phone ringing on the other end gave a boost to her spirits, as though already she were being connected to Dan in a way.

"O'Reilly's, this is Kelly. How can I help you?"

"You can get Dan James on the phone right away," Jenni said in an unsteady voice.

"Jenni? Is that you?"

"Yes, it's me." Her voice cracked slightly.

"What's wrong? Did your father lose the election?" Kelly asked sympathetically.

"Oh no, nothing like that. It's this whole mess with Brian. I just need to talk to Dan," Jenni replied in a defeated voice and added, "Would you go get him for me?"

"I can't," Kelly answered hesitantly. "He's gone."

"Gone?" Jenni questioned. The alarm in her voice was clear. "Gone where?"

"I don't know," Kelly answered honestly. "He checked out yesterday and didn't leave a forwarding address."

"Did he say anything? Anything at all?" Jenni felt a lump in her throat. Knowing she was very near to new tears, she bit hard on her lip.

"No. The fact is, I wasn't here when he checked out. He left the key, a bonus check for the staff, and nothing else," Kelly replied. "I don't know what to say, Jenni. I figured you knew all about it."

"No," Jenni said shaking her head. "I didn't." She felt the tears flow down her cheeks. "Look, Kelly, I don't feel like talking anymore. I need to pray, and just be alone. I hope you understand."

"Of course I understand. When will you be coming back?"

"It's too late to leave tonight. I guess I'll start back tomorrow. I have to find Dan."

After hanging up the phone, Jenni changed into her night clothes and sat down to write Brian a letter. For several moments she just looked at the piece of paper before her. What should she say? Should she tell him that she'd overheard the conversation? But what if that jeopardized her father's investigation?

"Dear Brian," she spoke the words out loud as she wrote them. "I can't marry you because I do not love you. I love Dan, and he has asked me to be his wife. I intend to marry him as soon as possible and would appreciate having no further relationship with you. I'm sorry if you think this is cold and calculated, but that is the way you seem to understand things best. Jennifer."

Having that task behind her, Jennifer knelt beside her bed and whispered a prayer. "Heavenly Father, I place myself completely in Your hands. Thank You for revealing Brian's true nature to me before I made a big mistake. Thank You for sending Dan my way and please help me to find him. Give me safety on my journey back to Colorado and help my parents to understand why I have to leave. I don't want to hurt them. Amen."

Jenni felt as if a weight had once again been lifted. She remembered the words that God have given her. Verses that showed her that the children of God would prove themselves, just as children of the devil would.

At the sound of a knock on her door, Jenni got quickly to her feet. "Who is it?"

"It's just me, honey."

"Daddy!" Jenni ran to unlock and open the door. "Oh, Daddy, I'm so glad you're here." Jenni fell into her father's arms and held him tightly.

"What's all this about?" Keith's concerned voice questioned.

"Oh, Daddy, you were so right about everything. Everything you said about Brian, Sonya, the whole works. You had everything pegged. Brian is going to try to ruin you."

Keith held his daughter at arms' length. "How do you know all of this?"

"I overheard him talking with Sonya this evening. He planned to marry me and use me to get at you." Jenni quickly spilled the entire story as her father listened quietly.

"And what do you plan to do about all of this?" her father finally questioned.

"I wrote Brian a goodbye letter and told him that I couldn't marry him because I love Dan James. I told him that I plan to marry Dan as soon as possible."

Keith raised a questioning eyebrow. "Is this true?"

Jenni looked up and smiled. "Yes, I do love Dan and I don't want to lose him. I plan to leave for home in the morning."

"You used to call this place home." The sadness in Keith Campbell's voice was evident.

"This will always be home to me—Daddy, but God's given me a very real choice and I'm making the right decision."

"I feel confident about it too. I don't really know why. I've never met this Dan James, but I have a feeling that he'll make a wonderful son-in-law," Jenni's father replied.

"I knew you'd understand. I love you so much," Jenni declared and quickly added, "You will be careful? I mean, about Brian."

"Brian is no threat to me, Jenni. I just received the proof I need this morning to have him disbarred. Would you like me to see to it that he gets your letter?"

"Please do. I'd really appreciate that." Jenni retrieved the letter and handed it to her father. "Thanks, Daddy."

"Sure thing, Princess."

twenty

Rounding a familiar bend, Jenni was rewarded with the distant view of Estes Park. She took the Highway 34 shortcut across the upper reach of Estes and avoided the downtown area. Within minutes she would pull into her old parking place and soon be sitting in front of her fireplace at O'Reilly's.

Minutes later, the dream had become a reality. Jenni had called Kelly from Loveland, and true to her word, Kelly had a fire and supper waiting for Jenni when she walked in.

"I've missed you and this place," Jenni sighed as she leaned back against the couch.

"I'm so glad to have you back. I hadn't realized how much I'd come to depend on your friendship until it was gone," Kelly said, handing Jenni a steaming bowl of chili.

"And here I thought you just liked me because I helped with the cleaning," Jenni teased. She tasted the chili and sighed again. "This is definitely worth driving six hundred miles for."

"Let's drop the pretense. Neither this bowl of chili or our friendship is the real reason you raced across Kansas today," Kelly said with a sly smile.

"I suppose it's too late to look for him tonight," Jenni rationalized.

"I suppose so," Kelly agreed.

"And I suppose that he hasn't called or let you know where he moved to."

"You're full of supposing tonight," Kelly said mischievously.

"I don't know why it took me so long to clear my brain and

realize that I've loved Dan from the first moment I laid eyes on him. Maybe even before that. I've always loved his writing and I feel that I've known a part of him forever," Jenni admitted.

"Sounds like a fairy tale romance if you ask me," Kelly grinned. She got up and put on her coat and hat. "Now that you're back, I really need to run into town for some things. Can you manage for a few minutes?"

"Oh, sure," Jenni lamented. "I've only been on the road since six this morning."

Kelly smiled. "Just remember the office is officially closed. If you lock up behind me, you shouldn't have to deal with any undesirables."

"Go on and get out of here before I change my mind," Jenni said with a laugh. She was glad to be home.

"Oh, by the way," Kelly said, handing Jenni a package wrapped in brown paper, "this came for you today."

Jenni put her chili on the table and took the package. "For me? Who's it from?"

"You know I don't snoop around your mail. Now if you don't mind, I'd better get to the store or they'll be closed." Kelly opened the door and said over her shoulder, "I'll see you later."

Jenni looked down at the package. The return address bore no name, but she recognized the handwriting instantly. "Dan!" she cried and tore open the brown wrapping.

Inside, to Jennifer's surprise was more wrapping. This paper was covered with balloons. Jenni more carefully undid the paper and slid the contents out to reveal yet another layer of wrapping. This was silver with bells on it, and Jenni knew it must be wedding shower paper. Her heart gave a lurch, and she held her breath as she unwrapped this last covering.

She smiled as she realized that she held Dan's newest novel in her hands. She had opened it with the jacket picture face up, and she smiled, remembering when her Aunt Pam had announced Dan's intent to stay at O'Reilly's. She had handed Jenni the book picture-side-up, making it an issue to point out Dan's good looks.

Jenni lingered over the photograph for a moment longer. It was her Dan all right. Sandy blond hair, parted on the side and combed over. Only Jenni knew how it fell forward when he laughed or how he ran his hand back through it when he was frustrated. Then there were the piercing eyes. Blue eyes so filled with a longing and passion for life that they threatened to engulf anyone close enough with their warmth and love.

Jenni found herself tracing the outline of the picture, as if to touch the man himself. Sighing, she turned the book over and gasped at the sight of the title.

"*Marry Me?*" she murmured. The title stood in bold red letters against a dark blue background. Below that was his name, "Daniel James" and far below that were two golden wedding bands entwined. Jenni looked for a letter or note that Dan might have added to accompany the book, but nothing revealed itself.

Gingerly, she opened the book, wondering if he had autographed it for her, but she found nothing on the inside of the cover or on the next page. Disappointed, Jenni continued to flip pages, until she came to the inside title page. There again was the large-lettered "Marry Me?", but beneath it something else caught Jenni's eye. Two words handwritten in ink stood out against the stark white of the paper. Two words that Dan James had written just for Jennifer Campbell.

Well? Dan.

Jenni gave a shout and jumped off the couch. "Yes! Yes! He still loves me! He still wants me to marry him!" She danced around the room before deciding to drive to the address given on the brown paper wrapper.

Carefully setting the precious book on the table, she dug through the wrapping paper until she came across the piece with the address. Grabbing her purse, Jenni wrestled it over her shoulder and reached for the door while trying to make out the address.

She took a couple of steps out the door and walked straight into Dan's warm embrace. "Dan!" she cried, but further words were hushed against his lips.

Jenni felt the piece of paper slip from her hand as her arms went around his neck. She returned his kiss with a matched longing that she'd scarcely known existed.

Dan pulled away abruptly, leaving Jenni, her eyes still closed, to fall slightly forward. She opened her eyes to find Dan's fiery blue eyes branding her very heart. She no longer doubted that she'd belong to him for the rest of her life. She silently thanked God for sending her a man to love. A man that loved her and loved God.

For a moment they stood in the silence of the softly falling snow. Physically, they were no longer touching, but in the depths of their souls, in the very most intimate part of their hearts, they were silently sharing a pledge that would bind them forever.

Jenni was the first to reach out, but Dan kept her at arms' length. "Well?" he grinned.

Jenni returned his smile. "Of course I'll marry you, Daniel James. Was there ever any doubt?"

Dan laughed heartily and pulled Jenni into his arms. "Welcome to our new life, Jennifer James," he murmured against her ear.

Jenni breathed in the crispness of the cold mountain air. "Jennifer James," she thought to herself. It did indeed have a nice ring to it.

A Letter To Our Readers

Dear Reader:

In order that we might better contribute to your reading enjoyment, we would appreciate your taking a few minutes to respond to the following questions. When completed, please return to the following:

Rebecca Germany, Editor
Heartsong Presents
P.O. Box 719
Uhrichsville, Ohio 44683

1. Did you enjoy reading *If Given a Choice*?
   ❏ Very much. I would like to see more books
      by this author!
   ❏ Moderately
      I would have enjoyed it more if _____

   _____

2. Are you a member of *Heartsong Presents*? Yes   No
   If no, where did you purchase this book? _____

   _____

3. What influenced your decision to purchase this
   book? (Check those that apply.)

   ❏ Cover   ❏ Back cover copy

   ❏ Title   ❏ Friends

   ❏ Publicity   ❏ Other _____

4. On a scale from 1 (poor) to 10 (superior), please rate the following elements.

___Heroine   ___Plot

___Hero   ___Inspirational theme

___Setting   ___Secondary characters

5. What settings would you like to see covered in *Heartsong Presents* books?

_____

_____

6. What are some inspirational themes you would like to see treated in future books?_____

_____

_____

7. Would you be interested in reading other *Heartsong Presents* titles?   ❏ Yes   ❏ No

8. Please check your age range:
❏ Under 18   ❏ 18-24   ❏ 25-34
❏ 35-45   ❏ 46-55   ❏ Over 55

9. How many hours per week do you read? ————

Name _____

Occupation _____

Address _____

City _____ State _____ Zip _____

Janelle Jamison

THE ALASKA TRILOGY

___*A Light in the Window*—Julie Eriksson returns to the Alaska territory to begin her career as a public health nurse. Her loneliness and discomfort is compounded by Sam Curtiss who persists in proposing a marriage that Julie fears would end her career. HP56 $2.95

___*Destiny's Road*—Beth Hogan has returned to Alaska a widow and mother of two young boys only to find her village overrun by builders of the Alcan Highway. Beth and her sons grow to love newcomer August Eriksson, but Beth knows she can never marry a man who is fighting God. HP71 $2.95

___*Iditarod Dream*—Mark Williams hopes to become more than Rita Eriksson's coach for the famed Iditarod race, but the walls that Rita has built around herself are too strong for human penetration. HP93 $2.95

....Hearts ♥ng....

.... Presents ....

Great Inspirational Romance at a Great Price!

Heartsong Presents books are inspirational romances in contemporary and historical settings, designed to give you an enjoyable, spirit-lifting reading experience. You can choose from 104 wonderfully written titles from some of today's best authors like Colleen L. Reece, Brenda Bancroft, Janelle Jamison, and many others.

When ordering quantities less than twelve, above titles are $2.95 each.

Hearts♥ng Presents
Love Stories Are Rated G!

That's for godly, gratifying, and of course, great! If you love a thrilling love story, but don't appreciate the sordidness of popular paperback romances, **Heartsong Presents** is for you. In fact, **Heartsong Presents** is the *only inspirational romance book club*, the only one featuring love stories where Christian faith is the primary ingredient in a marriage relationship.

Sign up today to receive your first set of four, never before published Christian romances. Send no money now; you will receive a bill with the first shipment. You may cancel at any time without obligation, and if you aren't completely satisfied with any selection, you may return the books for an immediate refund!

Imagine. . .four new romances every month—two historical, two contemporary—with men and women like you who long to meet the one God has chosen as the love of their lives. . .all for the low price of $9.97 postpaid.

To join, simply complete the coupon below and mail to the address provided. **Heartsong Presents** romances are rated G for another reason: They'll arrive *Godspeed!*